P9-EET-439

25 AUG 2011

HULL CREEK

JIM NICHOLS
HULL CREEK
A NOVEL
Down East

This novel is a work of fiction. All characters appearing in this work are fictitious. Any resemblance to real individuals, living or dead, is purely coincidental. While some of the landscapes, communities, and businesses may be actual places, or based on actual places, the events portrayed in this novel and the actions of the characters in these places are entirely fictitious.

Cover photograph © Dean Abramson

Designed by Lynda Chilton

ISBN 978-0-89272-915-9

Printed in the United States

Down East
BOOKS·MAGAZINE·ONLINE
www.downeast.com

Distributed to the trade by National Book Network

Library of Congress Cataloging-in-Publication Information available on request

ONE

When I traded in my old man's boat I kept his brown box radio, put it on a shelf on the port wall of the wheelhouse. Now Polky's spinning the dial, trying to find a station as we motor through the dark. But there's only static, so he shuts it back off. He rips another beer out of the plastic six-pack rings, pops the top.

"So how much did you pay for this battleship?" he says.

"Enough."

"And you couldn't have a half decent sound system put in?"

"Ollsen doesn't do sound systems."

"All right," Polky says. "I guess I don't check tomorrow's weather."

"Chance of fog," I say.

He laughs. "Just what you need, huh? On top of poor fishing."

"And a lousy price to boot." I shake my head at the way things have been going. Cool air slips through the *Julie Marie*'s wheelhouse. It's full evening now, we've moved offshore and out of the fog and we can see the stars, clumped in rich clusters against a deep black sky.

"She rides nice," Polky says. "I'll give you that."

"She does."

"You happy with the wood?"

"I never liked a glass boat," I say.

"Lot easier to keep up."

"I hate the way they bob around, though."

We climb over deep swells, unable to see the mainland lights because of the fog trapped against the shore by cool ocean air. It makes the gulf seem big around us; makes me nervous about trusting the compass. At least we'll be able to see the Marine Patrol though, unless they get tricky. I feel my stomach shrink again at what we're doing, and I turn to watch Polky walk aft, put a foot up on the transom, and give a little hop to settle his balance. It's strange to have him on my boat. Usually I only see him in town, or at the lobster pound, sometimes at my house. I turn back, check my watch: nine o'clock. We slip along and I feel what a nice boat she is in the way she holds herself in the water.

Polky comes back, smelling like a cigarette.

"Making good time," I tell him.

He looks at his watch, which he wears under the wrist, like me.

I tap out a beat on the wheel with my fingers. We ride along and Polky looks at me a few times, drinks his beer. Finally he smirks and says, "So how do you like being a bad-ass?"

"Is that what I am?" I say.

"You're a bad-ass in training."

"Keep dreaming," I say.

"You'll come around," he says. "It's in your blood."

"Bullshit."

Polky holds up his beer. "Your grandfather ran this stuff."

"Booze is different," I say.

"It's the same thing," Polky says. When I don't answer he snorts and goes quiet. But I know he'll bring it up again. He truly believes that smuggling is all right. You can't go by the rules, he says, because nobody else does. Especially not the assholes who make up the rules. I guess it's all in how you look at it. I can't imagine my grandfather running drugs. But alcohol was an illegal drug back then, wasn't it? I think this over and decide I'd better stop making Polky's arguments for him. I should try doing something useful instead, like maybe checking our course. We've changed our heading to run across the mouth of the Bay of Fundy toward the southwest end of Nova Scotia, and because of the huge tidal flow in and out of the bay you have to watch out.

ooooo

We're back in the fog at eleven o'clock, and a half hour later we slow to motor in to the little town of Stewartville, making for Griffin's dock around a point from the town landing. It's pretty dark, but eventually I see a spotlight shining off the dull-red fuel pump at the end of the dock. There's a stack of wire lobster traps on the other end and I see bait shacks running back into the yard. Unlike Pequot, this still looks like a working harbor. I bring the *Julie Marie* in against the float, and after we work the lines, Polky pops another beer and hands it over—his way of telling me to stay put.

"Be right back," he says.

I sit on a crate while Polky scuffs up the dirt drive to the little house on the hill behind the wharf. Around the waterfront the fog hangs on everything. A foghorn sounds and the water rustles against the shore. Up the hill I can hear Polky knock, and after a minute or two the door opens and I hear the faint rumble of their voices. Then the door shuts and Polky walks back down.

"He's got it in the shed." He holds up a key.

We spend the next hour lugging duty-free rope to the boat, tossing it aboard. Then we take a minute to catch our breath. The deck is covered with the heavy strapped coils, not a real lucrative cargo, but you can make twenty bucks or so on each coil and since the geniuses in Washington decided we needed sinking line, everybody's got to change out. I'm hoping to get a boat payment out of it. We go up the hill to the house and Griffin—maybe fifty, with gray stuck-up hair—opens the door and points into the living room. He follows us in with a pot of hot tea laced with whiskey.

"*Irish* whiskey," he says, with a bit of lilt in his voice. "We'll drink to your ill-gotten gains. We'll drink to the poor, deluded tax man."

Polky shrugs. "What he don't know won't hurt him."

We take the couch and he sits in a rocking chair, crossing his legs and raising his teacup. We sip the tea and talk things over, trying to be quiet about it so we won't wake up his wife. He says that he personally thinks lobster fishing is going to hell in a hand basket. And trying to supplement your income is getting harder all the time, too. Just the past week the local Mountie told him they were keeping an eye on him. "He called me a gangster!" Griffin says with a laugh. "Said I ought to get out of it while I still could. Told him I would if I had a choice in the matter."

"You're being watched?" Polky says.

Griffin grins. "No worries, Billy; strictly office hours with those birds."

Polky grunts and looks out the near window.

"Go to work in the *service sector*," I tell him. "That's what they want in Maine. Work in the service sector and keep the tourists happy."

Griffin says, "There's that, isn't there?"

"Fucking *swanks!*" Polky mutters.

Griffin says he's a part-time carpenter, and he supposes he could try that full time. But he doesn't really want to pound nails for a living. I tell how I went to school for a couple semesters, but had to come back and work the grounds when my father got hurt and couldn't haul.

"Ah yes," Griffin says. "Use 'em or lose 'em."

"I can't believe it's been ten years, though."

"A fucking decade," Polky says.

"Time flies, eh?" Griffin says.

We sit there and finish off the pot of tea. Then Polky stands up. We troop back to the kitchen and put our cups in the sink. Griffin tells us not to worry about being quiet, his wife would probably sleep through Armageddon. "All part of marriage to a gangster," he says with a grin. He follows us down the path to the dock and unlocks the gas pump. He fuels the boat and begins filling my extra cans. The pump clicks as its numbers change and the gas rushes into the containers until Griffin releases the trigger. He hangs the spigot up, takes out a pocket calculator, figures how much we owe him in Canadian and then converts it to American money.

"Pay the man," Polky says.

I hand over most of my lobster money from that afternoon.

"A pleasure," Griffin says. "You bloody gangsters."

We board the *Julie Marie* and Griffin throws the lines in. "You might watch out on the way back," he says. "I understand they nabbed one of the Jonesport boys yesterday."

"What was he doing?"

Griffin just smiles.

"We'll watch out," Polky says.

Griffin heads back up the hill. Polky tells me to hold it a minute and climbs out onto the foredeck to take down the maroon and white buoy, the one you have to display so the Marine Patrol will know you're hauling your own traps. He swings back into the wheelhouse and says, "No sense advertising." Then he looks thoughtful. "We could tack a blanket over the stern. You got a blanket below?"

"No," I say.

"You got anything?"

"Just some rags," I say.

"Christ," he says and shakes his head.

Considering this kind of stuff makes me feel funny all over again, but I don't say anything. I push the boat away from the dock and we make out through the fog, circling the point. Running slow, the motor smooth, we head for open water. After a mile or so I open her up and take a course across the bay toward the mainland.

"Want me to steer awhile?" Polky says.

"I'm okay. Go on down and take the bunk."

"That's all right." He sits on the floor with his back to the bulkhead, his arms crossed and his leather jacket pulled tight around him. He goes to sleep in about two minutes. He wouldn't take the bunk because that would be soft, but he doesn't mind sleeping while I steer.

I'm a little drunk, and lulled by the rhythm of the engine and the feel of the swells, my mind wanders back along the ten years since I came home from school. Three hundred traps at first, all the old man would fish because back then they called you a hog if you set more. But that gradually changed, and you had to set more to keep up. More traps and less money. In trouble with the bank, too. Still a bloody fisherman in spite of everything, though I sometimes wish I could have finished school and gotten a real job. But that was just never an option.

My thoughts drift farther back and I'm a boy, knitting trap heads, painting buoys, happy to be old enough to help. I'm sternmanning, running in with the old man's big hand on my shoulder. I'm taking my own hand-me-down dory out to the few dozen traps I'm allowed to haul on my own, proud to have the gulls flocking along behind just like they did with the grownups. I see it all, right up to the accident that killed my mother and left my father too beat up to work and too sad to care. Then I'm brought back by Polky's chain-saw snoring, and I snap to and the first thing I do is check the compass. But we're on course, I've steered automatically. I rub my eyes, clear my throat, and lean out into the cool air to spit over the side past the snatch block.

Polky's snore breaks off, and he sits up.

"Sleeping Beauty," I say.

He looks around, then pats himself down to see if he's all there. Making sure I didn't steal his wallet, maybe. He grunts and gets to his feet, rubbing his chin and mouth. He turns his wrist to check the time.

"We're getting there," I say. I bring the bow around, heading on a tangent to home.

He yawns like a moose. "What'd you do, steer all night?"

"It wasn't too bad."

"Should have woke me, Troy."

"You looked too cute snoozing."

Polky snorts. "So you decide where you're going to dump it?"

"Right in Owls Head, I guess."

He nods and walks aft, picking his way through the rope. It's gloomy ahead. Drops are collecting on the windshield, running upwards in little streams.

"Here comes the fog," I say.

"None too soon, either," Polky says darkly.

I twist around and see the running lights of a small boat, maybe three miles off, coming our way fast.

Polky walks back into the wheelhouse.

"Who is it?" I say.

"Who do you think?"

I don't answer. I know who it must be.

"Well?" Polky says.

Choices fly through my mind, but I can't seem to slow them down long enough to take a good look. Polky waits just so long, then reaches past me and shoves the throttle. The *Julie Marie* leaps ahead and I stumble before grabbing the wheel. I don't bother to argue, just tweak our heading. We're swallowed up pretty quickly. I change course again and run along blind. Then, when we're well into it, I throttle back, feel the *Julie Marie* settle lower in the water.

"I hope you know what we're doing," I say.

"Can you hear them?"

"No."

"Cut the engine."

I cut the engine and we drift, rising and falling. Polky grabs my arm and points. I see the spotlight stabbing into the fog and I'm surprised they're this close. Then their engine goes idle, and somebody says in a high voice through a bullhorn: "*Attention, lobster boat in the area! Please set your VHF radio to channel sixteen. Listen for instructions! This is the Marine Patrol, and we are conducting a routine search of all vessels!*"

"Sure," Polky mutters. "We'll get right on that."

"*Attention!*" comes the voice again. "*Your cooperation is mandatory! Please set your VHF radio to channel sixteen and listen for instructions! We intend to board and search your vessel! Refusal to follow instructions may result in legal action including the possible loss of your vessel!"*

"Well?" I say.

"They'd have to fight the bank for her anyway."

"Good point." I wait until they're running again, then push the starter button, throw the *Julie Marie* into gear and give her full throttle. It's exciting, what we're doing. I feel it in my gut. We charge away from the Marine Patrol and run all out into the fog until the spotlight disappears behind us. I watch the compass, check the bottom finder, but it's deep out here.

"Maybe we should put it overboard," I say to Polky.

"Last resort," Polky says. "You need the money too bad."

"Their boat's faster."

"You've got the jump on them," Polky says. "And you ain't going anywhere in a straight line."

"What if they have me on radar?"

"You can't see a little wood boat on radar unless you're awful good."

"What if they're awful good?"

"Not that crowd." Polky grins.

After ten minutes I cut the engine again. We drift, rocking. I stare around at the dense fog, half expecting the Marine Patrol boat to come busting into sight. Then I hear their engine. They're not so close any more. When a foghorn sounds I restart and set off on a different course. The voice over the bullhorn follows us, but I can't hear what it's saying any more. It gets fainter every time I shut the boat down, and finally I can't hear them at all.

Polky says, "Now he'll head for shore."

"You think he knows us?"

"He bushwacked us, didn't he?"

"Maybe."

"I'd forget Owls Head, anyway."

"Where, then?"

"How about the Number Two Point?" Polky's eyes are bright. The old blood is flowing. I know what he feels like now, and that scares me a little. It's too much like when we played basketball, competitive like that. I shove the *Julie Marie* into gear and as I feed her the gas my heart speeds up, too. I shake my head, staring into the fog, wondering how I came to be out here in the middle of the night, smuggling rope, dodging the clam cops.

TWO

I guess I can figure the day it all changed. I remember coming in, upset after another poor haul, yanking the skiff toward the old iron bridge that takes Seaview Street out of town and bends it down the south Pequot peninsula. It was late in the afternoon, not a cloud in the sky, and I had my eyes on my lobster boat, moored on the east side in front of Danny Brinker's marina. Then I stopped to look over my shoulder. The sun was low and bright, flashing down the creek, turning the water under the bridge the color of a new penny. I stirred with one oar to change my heading, then bent back to it. When I reached the bridge the current drove me sideways, but I dug harder and slowly made headway.

Understand, I didn't *have* to work that hard.

I could have climbed out and walked the skiff up the narrows. There were foot rocks all along the bank. But I was just too pissed off. I had that helpless feeling that things were happening I couldn't control, but one thing I *could* do was lean on those bloody oars.

It was cool under the bridge, only May and the air still a bit raw, but coming out the other side the sun warmed my neck as I inched along to smoother water. In two more deep strokes I was clear, and I slowed to catch my breath and looked around at the new growth on the high banks: the spring greens, the clumps of pink and purple phlox. It was pretty, peaceful, and I lost a little of my crankiness.

But I was still worried. Who wouldn't be?

I started in pulling again, past black rock tops and through a wooded bend that brought the upper creek into view. I swung around on the thwart, careful not to tip—it was a small skiff and I'm a pretty big guy—and switched hands on the oars so I could face forward to check out the birds. The whole upper creek was alive because of the alewive run. There were gulls on the rocks, a fish hawk high up in a tree, a big mess of shags in the water with just their long black necks showing.

The shags backed away as I drew close and then sort of levitated to sprint along the surface, beating their wings and pattering their webbed feet on the water, raising a racket that in the confines of the creek sounded exactly like a roomful of applause.

It was a noise I'd heard every spring of my life.

I watched them go and thought of the old man. When the birds took off like this, he would bow his head like they were clapping for him and say, "Thank you, thank you very much," his Elvis imitation so lame you couldn't help laughing.

I smiled despite myself, watching the shags strain up into the air. They're piss-poor flyers. I think it's the set of their wings that makes them seem to work so hard. You look at the gulls and their wings are forward compared to the shags, and you have to admit they're much better flyers, no matter what else you might think of them, which isn't much in my case.

The shags lifted over the pine trees and birches, the gulls circled back toward the harbor and I caught a quick sight of the fish hawk pounding away north, looking a lot like a giant gull.

But he was no dump bird. He was a working guy, like me.

I pushed on up the creek, my farmhouse approaching behind the tall trees. The old place was built before the Civil War, but was still sturdy and warm, with a wide deck I'd added myself back when I had a little money in my pocket, before I somehow turned into just another dub lobster fisherman.

About here I told myself to quit whining.

But I couldn't help wondering if I should have kept the old man's boat a couple more seasons. Problem was I'd had a little money, and I'd wanted an Ollsen boat bad. Old man Ollsen was getting ready to retire, so I went for it.

I drifted up to the old dock, weathered and warped, built and rebuilt from the time when we Hulls hauled traps by hand, from dories in close to shore, when you didn't have to chase the bugs around. I'd heard the stories since I was old enough to listen: how you could pick them from behind rocks at low tide, how they'd caught millions of pounds for the canneries, no size limits, no worrying about berried females, no problems.

On the dock I arched my back, something out of whack in there. All the old-timers had bad backs, and I supposed that was in store for me, too, assuming I could fish long enough to become an old timer.

I stretched until my spine popped back into place. Then, instead of heading straight to the house, I walked out into the field that followed the creek. It had been a while since I'd been up here. I kicked through the grass to the woods and walked along the overgrown mule trail to the earthwork that blocked an old canal from the creek. I climbed up the slant and looked in. It was pretty wet, because this time of year the canal still diverted water from just below Seven Tree Pond. Come summer, that skim-off would stop, the water would sink into the ground, and grass and weeds would cover the bottom. It had been that way since they quit logging years ago.

I remembered playing in the dried-up canal bed, using it for a hideout with the rest of the gang: Niki Harjula, Billy Polky, Danny Brinker. Thinking of those days made me smile: how we'd steal around town in the evening, peeping in windows, eavesdropping, and then dash back to the canal. Back then we thought the whole town belonged to us.

I fished through the old memories for a while, then backed down the slant and walked out of the woods. I headed back across the field toward the house, noticing the shags were back: two or three hundred watching from the creek. I crossed a stretch of lawn that wound past cedars, birches, and the small bog with the frog pond, stopping to check the fiddleheads hatching out of their little mounds. I remembered my mother harvesting them for supper greens, and the sadness welled up in me like it still does sometimes.

Then I thought about Julie Marie.

I missed her, too, but it was different. She wasn't dead, for one thing. And it was more of an indoor feeling: I missed her in the kitchen, the living room, the shower she'd use for an hour at a time. The bedroom, too, in a way that was so messed up I couldn't even bring myself to sleep in our old bed any more.

But I didn't miss her outdoors. She wasn't connected to the property the way my parents were. It had never been anything special to her. It was no great shakes, for example, that we didn't have neighbors close by.

Hell, she *liked* neighbors!

Missing Julie Marie—her red hair, her smart mouth, her flat belly, and freckled breasts—I walked up the driveway, grabbed the bills and flyers from the dinged-up mailbox, came back through the shed. There were buoys in there, tools and trap-making materials, too, snowshoes, a cracked baseball bat, a hand-mower, a grill and bag of charcoal, my old Schwinn, covered with cobwebs and missing its rear tire, a stack of *National Geographics,* a hoe, rake, and shovel leaning against the wall, a rickety bookcase full of the old man's paperbacks. I picked one up and opened to a turned-down page. I pictured him in his recliner, reading with his mouth open. Catching flies, my mother called it, but he was just lost in the words. People think folks like us don't read, but my old man would read anything: books, newspapers, magazines, cereal boxes. I'd caught it from him, and I still remember how my teachers made a big deal out of a *fisherman's* kid reading at lunch time!

I set the book down and looked at a box full of hardcover textbooks. Sometimes I thought I should just toss them, but once in while I came back from Captain Cobb's Crow's Nest with a little clip going, and I'd pick up *Fishes of the Gulf of Maine,* with this big, weird flounder on the cover. I had hoped to study marine biology at Maine, and sometimes the old textbooks still made that seem possible. But mostly they just sat, collecting dust and bat droppings.

I left the shed and headed for the kitchen.

There I picked through the mail, still thinking about my folks and Julie Marie. I saw the logo of a three-masted schooner and tore the envelope open and read: . . . *late payments . . . may find it necessary to observe the terms of your loan* . . . and my face turned hot. I looked around for something to smash, but there was nothing handy. I could've punched a hole in the wall, but the last time I hit a stud and broke a goddamn knuckle.

I jammed the letter into my pocket and yelled: "God-damned *assholes!*" Which was mostly just letting off steam, but still, I was wound up. I stomped out to my pickup, noting the cluster of rust spots across the cab, like somebody had sprayed it with a machine gun a few years back. When I fired it up I thought it ran all right for an old piece of crap, and the tailgate still latched despite a constellation of dents. Yeah, I thought, backing onto the street, maybe you should have made the old boat work for a little while longer, you big, dumb genius you.

THREE

I drove down Hull Street and at the stop sign looked sideways at Charlie Hamalainen's house. It was the last of the old Capes that used to sit around the harbor and now it sat boarded-up on the only plot of land I didn't own from the bridge on up. There were still plenty of the old names around, the Finns and Swedes who settled the area, but I was pretty much the last to live near the water. I swung the pickup left and drifted down Seaview, past fancy new houses to where the town puckered in a five-way square. Traffic moved through the square thick enough to keep me waiting.

I finally nosed out in front of a convertible Saab driven by a woman with a red scarf around her neck and her chin in the air. She gave me a look, and when I answered with the old single-digit, her eyes widened. She turned them straight ahead and didn't look at me again.

I steered through the brick downtown and stopped at a crosswalk by the village green to let a family of tourists stroll across the street, lapping triple-scoop ice cream cones. I saw they'd put the big flag up in the green for Memorial Day. The flag went limp, wrapping itself around the pole, and I thought about Julie Marie again. I remembered before things went bad, how she would ride close beside me with her hand on my leg. I'd get a little worked up and she'd keep me that way with a touch here, a scratch there until we got home, or, if I was real lucky, until she told me to pull over somewhere.

The tourists reached the other side and I headed off through a stretch of white houses with black shutters, where most of the leftover natives lived: Pulkinins, Ericksons, Lehtinens, Hokkenens.

Their homes were all Capes, with fenced-in gardens and scallop-shingled sheds and scenes painted on their mailboxes. Some of them had home-made saunas out back.

I cruised through the town's only stoplight just as it blinked yellow, then flew down a long grade to the shopping center. There was a grocery store, an auto parts shop, and a Chinese restaurant. A health food store, hobby shop, and a UPS store. They all had mansard roofs, brown shingles, and flower gardens.

When I parked opposite the Pequot Savings and Loan a little yellow VW pulled in tight against my front bumper. I got out and stared: there were plenty of empty spaces, no need to make me back and fill when I left. Then I saw who it was and I had to laugh. Niki Harjula climbed out and stood there grinning. She was short and sturdy and had wicked blue eyes. She still looked a lot like my childhood pal, only dressed like a grown-up, with a tan blazer, a long reddish skirt, high-heeled boots. And she had a haircut right out of some fancy magazine, cropped short as a boy's, sort of jumbled around. I liked how it set off her cheekbones and wide, pretty mouth.

"Hey, poopsie," Niki said.

I laughed again. "New car?"

"New to me." She turned to shut the door, and for a second I understood why the suits had been after her. She wasn't bad to look at, and they'd never seen her playing in the creek in her overalls, with mud on her face and a soup-bowl haircut. They'd never heard her say from next to them in their bed: "Troy? Does your daddy ever strap you?"

Niki was always popping up at our house. I remember once when we were on the way to Seven Tree Pond, and her face just sort of appeared in the pickup's rear window. I remember the old man doing a double-take, then rolling his eyes at my mother and saying, "How many goddamn kids did you say we had?" But then he laughed and pulled over so I could join Niki for the rest of the ride. Kids could ride in the back of pickups in those days, just like dogs.

"How'd you get here?" I asked her when we were rolling again.

"I come up when you wasn't looking," she said. "And I snuck right in!" Now Niki cocked her head at me and said, "You worked up about something, Troy Hull?"

"It shows?"

She just gave me a look.

"Well, it's your piece-of-shit boss," I said.

"Keith?"

"None other."

She circled the car and we crossed toward the bank. It was cooling off, the sun down behind the trees. Inside, Niki headed around the counter and I waited at her window, looking at her stuffed animals, her little flower calendar, a Red Cross piggy bank beside her nameplate, a Nicaraguan Children's Fund mini-poster, a UNICEF brochure, a Greenpeace card in a brass frame.

She walked up and nodded at my envelope. "So what's that?"

"A little love-note from the Dump Bird."

Niki took a quick look to see if Keith Zeiglaar was around. Keith was another one who used to come up the street to play. We put up with him because his parents gave him cool presents like a Rawlings infielder's glove or an NFL football. Not that he'd been able to use them very well: in high school he was the kid who brought the oranges at half-time and took care of our dirty uniforms. We called him the Zeagull. "Look out!" we'd say, "hide your French fries!" But Keith's folks sent him away to Tufts and he got to be a big shot when he came home. You didn't laugh at him any more if he might happen to see you.

Niki held out her hand. "Gimme."

I handed her the note.

Niki scanned it. "Oh, Troy!"

"Yeah, no shit," I said.

"Have you got an appointment?" she said, and when I shook my head she walked down to the office and knocked on the door. She came back and told me Keith would see me in a minute. Then she smiled like she was embarrassed. I understood: imagine, ending up with Keith Zeiglaar for your frigging boss.

Her face went sad then.

"What?" I said.

"I was sorry to hear about you and Julie Marie," she said. "I tried to call you up a couple of times."

"That's okay, I wasn't answering the phone."

"I probably should have come over."

"Wasn't answering the door, either." I laughed, but it really wasn't my favorite subject. Niki looked at me, her eyes so blue, and I remembered my mother framing her face, saying: "Niki Harjula, you have the *prettiest* peepers," and how Niki—who might have been six at the time—grinned like a monkey. She wasn't used to compliments.

"Have you heard from her at all?" Niki said now.

"Not since she said she was filing."

"She still in town?"

"Naw, they moved up the coast."

A guy in a trench coat came into the lobby, and I stepped aside to let Niki wait on him. The guy smiled at Niki like he thought he was charming her. She smiled back like she did with everyone. Then Keith Zeiglaar stuck his fat face out the office door and said, "Come on down, Troy," before disappearing back into his hidey-hole.

FOUR

I felt like I was back in school, walking down to the principal's office. And when I saw Keith still had his high school pictures on the wall, the feeling was even stronger. Keith was on the phone and he pointed to the straight-back chair beside his desk. I sat down and looked at the shot of the Pequot cheerleaders that hung above his filing cabinet. They all had short ponytails high on their heads. Julie Marie was in the exact center, one hand on her hip and the other raised in a fist. She had a wide smile and you could see how bright-eyed she was. I looked at her and missed her like hell. Then I remembered what she'd done to me and my face went hot: damn Scandinavian skin. Or Scandahoovian, as my mother used to say.

Keith said, "That's dynamite, sir!" into the phone.

It made me cringe listening to him suck up. I looked back at the picture of the cheerleaders, at Niki Harjula in the front row, and I remembered how excited she was to be picked. I remembered how she had all the moves, but not that pretend *wantonness*. Which was ironic, seeing as how she would drop out and marry the biker boy within a couple of months.

Keith said, "You are an awesome cat, sir!"

"Jesus, Keith," I said. I couldn't help it.

He turned his back on me. I looked at the wall again. Next to the cheerleader picture was the hoop team. Bill Polky and I were in the front row, holding a basketball between us. *Eastern Maine Champs* was written on the ball, with the date and score of the game. Polky was mugging as usual, and I had the dumb look I always end up with in photographs. Keith was there in his sport coat, a head shorter than the ballplayer beside him, looking down his nose like he was important, his bangs sitting on the top of his glasses.

Keith hung up the phone and swung back. He still had the bangs, but they didn't reach to his gold-rims, and they were turning prematurely gray.

I held the note out and said, "What the hell is this?"

"Well hi, Troy!" he said. "Nice to see you, too!"

"Come on, Keith." I dropped the note on his desk.

Keith pressed the note flat and stared at it. "Well," he said, "it's your late payments, Troy."

"What's so different this time?"

"Troy," he smiled at me like he had a toothache. "You've had six in a row."

"You know what the fishing's been like."

"You're supposed to *plan* for that, aren't you?" Keith said. "Save your nuts for winter and all that?" He tapped the note and frowned. To me he looked like somebody *pretending* to be a banker. But other people took him seriously enough. Come Memorial Day he'd be sweating through his sport coat, marching through town with the rest of the big shots, tossing candy to the kids. He shook his head. "I'm sorry, Troy," he said, "it's just that we have a more involved board of directors these days. They don't want us doing business the old *laissez-faire* way any more." He looked at me, and for a second I thought he was going to explain what *laissez-faire* meant, like we were back in school and he was the class brain and I was someone who needed help. But he didn't, he went on with this bright expression. "Listen," he said, "have you given any more thought to *selling* your property? Weren't you and Julie considering it at one point?"

"*Julie* was considering it," I told him.

"Well, don't take this wrong, but maybe you ought to consider it again?"

"It's Hull Creek, Keith," I said.

"I realize that. But if you can't pay your mortgage . . ."

"Back up a little," I said. "You remember we talked all this stuff out, right?"

"I don't remember saying it was okay to miss payments."

"But I haven't *missed* any payments."

"Actually, technically speaking, you have," Keith said. "You've overlapped, which is pretty much the same as missing them." He gave me the same old shrug, like none of this was his fault.

"I asked you back then about slack fishing," I said.

"And I gave you the best answer I could."

"You said you'd work with me."

Keith just waved that off. "We don't remember it quite the same way, Troy. But that's okay, that's why we have a contract in writing. I can dig that out, if you want."

"I know what the contract says."

"Well, it's pretty clear about paying in a timely manner."

I was sitting up straight by now. I could remember Keith joking about the legal stuff, saying that I shouldn't worry, it was just to get it past the bean-counters. I remembered how it was snowing outside, how I'd had a fall of hauling like never before—three, four pounds a trap, day after day—and it had convinced me to take the plunge. I remembered how Keith had brought me in to this same office and brushed off his overcoat and hung it on the coat rack and sat down, and I remembered how eager he was to sign me up.

"This is total bullshit," I said.

"It's just business, Troy." Keith gave me the *blameless* face again and made a big production out of frowning down at his fancy watch. "Listen," he said, and he stood up and tugged his sport coat down. "I wish I had more time." He nodded at the phone. "That was the chamber president. Big doings!" He laughed and squinted at me, like we were still high school buddies. "You know about *American Road* coming to town?"

I didn't say anything, but he went on as if I had.

"Well, they're high maintenance!" he said. "But stuff like this really puts Pequot on the map." Keith started around the desk, waving a hand in the air. "But I don't want you to worry about that notice, Troy," he said. "It's generated by computer, and half the time we don't even know they're going out!" He stuck out his hand, and I shook it, mostly because of all those oranges and towels and sweaty uniforms. But then Keith said, "All the same, I would think about testing the market. You've got a beautiful piece of property there, and we both know this isn't a fisherman's town any more. You could go back to school, make something of yourself."

I dropped his hand. "Make something of myself?"

"You know what I mean. We'd have to be involved, of course, because you're technically in default on the mortgage . . . "

"I'm in default?"

"Technically speaking."

"Jesus, this gets better and better."

"It's more communication than anything," Keith said. "Don't let it bother you! But maybe think a little about the market . . ."

"I'd burn it down first," I said.

"Well, that wouldn't be very smart."

I bit my tongue to keep from saying something else that wouldn't be very smart, and then walked out of the office. Keith came hustling after me, saying, "Troy, Troy!" He caught me at the door—I would have had to make it into a dumb-ass race to avoid it—and said, "Troy, please!" He was puffing a little, and his voice had gone up an octave. "Keep in mind, it's just business!" he said. "Sometimes it's nothing more than a way to keep someone on their toes!" He took hold of my arm, but I shook loose and went out the door and across the parking lot and swung into the pickup. I started it and sat there fuming with my hand on the gearshift. Finally I put it in reverse to back away from Niki's little car, but just as I did she came out of the building and I shut the engine off. She hurried over, one hand on her blouse the way girls do to keep their breasts from jumping around.

I leaned over and opened the door.

She stepped up and in, a little stiffly because of her skirt. She pulled the door shut and looked at me with her eyes open wide. "Listen, Troy," she said, "I've only got a second. Do you know who Trace White is?"

"I've heard the name."

"Major trust-fund baby? Bought that magazine and sold it out of state?"

I remembered *that*, all right. It was a boating magazine, started by some local guys. They'd hit some rough sledding and Trace had offered to buy in out of the goodness of his blue-blooded heart. Which was fine until a year later, when he sold the whole kit and caboodle to some outfit in Massachusetts. There'd been a big fuss, people writing letters to the editor, and I remembered he'd written one back: *Don't people around here understand business decisions?*

"What about him?" I said.

"He's the new board member." Niki made *board member* sound like *asshole*.

"Great," I said. "Perfect."

"Just so you know," she touched my arm, opened the door. I watched her walk back into the bank with a thought or two about asking her out. But it was hard to get all the way past the old feeling. And suppose we did hit it off and she wanted to jump into bed; I wasn't sure I was ready for *that*. Not after Julie Marie. I wasn't exactly brimming with confidence. But Niki did have a wicked splendid ass. Polky said once that if you took her clamming, sat her down and rocked her in the mudflat, it would leave a perfect impression of a valentine.

I backed out of the parking space and drove out and along Main Street to the stoplight. I sat there staring at my hometown. There was the rocky mountaintop with a stone tower—all that was left of an old hotel—and, to the right, a cliff sheering down into trees. A green hill led from there down to the town, with brick buildings, two white church steeples, and a dozen gulls swirling over the waterfront like they owned the damn place. It was a pretty sight, but I was in a bad humor and couldn't appreciate it. And I stayed that way. From that point on I was ready to test the waters with Polky. It just took him a little while to ask me.

FIVE

We move in slow through the fog until the Owls Head Light shows, and then I nudge the throttle and we run along until the light disappears. Long swells lift us broadside, rocking us, pushing us toward the mainland. I let them ease us in closer, the engine a touch above idle, until I hear the surf on the rocks, then see the misty trees only a few yards away. Then I turn and run along the shore until I reach the big round boulder atop the ledge at Number Two Point. We follow the channel around the point into a little cove, rumored to have been a smuggler's cove. There are sunken logs and big rocks that make it tricky inside, so maybe the rumors are true. We tiptoe in past the debris and I shut her off and throw out the anchor. We listen hard, but there's nothing.

"Okay, let's get to it," Polky says.

A half-hour later I swing the last coil of rope over the side. There's a splash and the warp sinks down out of sight. We stand still, listening to the surf, to a foghorn somewhere. I climb up on the roof and reattach the buoy. Then I swing down, start the engine and steer out of the cove, around the point, and across the next cove and along the shore for half a mile until we see the lighthouse beacon. I pick my way through lobster boats and cars into Owls Head harbor. It's not even five o'clock. Even the gulls are still in bed. When I can see fog drifting past the spotlight on Cormier's wharf, I reverse engine, let the boat ease up to the float. When the bow touches I bring the stern in tight. Polky steps up on the rail, lunges over. "You want to come over for breakfast?" he says from the float.

"I would if you could cook."

He grins at me, gives me a half-assed salute, then turns and hauls himself up the ladder. When he stops short of the top, I look up: someone's standing above him, one hand on the hoist. Polky lets himself back down, comes over to the boat, and says, "Clam cops" out the side of his mouth. I don't need him to tell me that: the first Marine Patrol officer is already stepping backwards onto the float, and the second guy is halfway down the ladder. I take a closer look at the second guy and realize that's a female ass in the dark green pants and I roll my eyes at Polky.

He's spotted her, too. "Don't tell me," he says.

We've heard about this new clam cop, her name is Tracy Thibeault. She's supposed to have a bad attitude; guys are already calling her Dickless Tracy. I hold the *Julie Marie* steady as they come over in their windbreakers and ball caps. It's Don Moody in the lead, a hefty guy with a handlebar mustache who used to fish before going into law enforcement, which makes him a hard guy to put anything past.

"Troy," Don says. He looks at Polky.

"Don," I say. "What brings you out?"

"I might ask you the same." He puts his hands on the rail and peers into the boat. He turns his big head, looking around. The other officer comes up beside him, working the Marine Patrol cap around on her head. Don Moody pushes off the rail and says, "This here is Officer Thibeault."

"Gentlemen," she says. She's stocky, medium height, kind of pretty, with red cheeks, dark eyes, thin lips. She doesn't look very friendly, and I remember the stories.

Moody turns back to me. "So how about it?"

"No big deal. I wanted Billy to listen to my engine before I went out this morning. Been having some trouble with it. Didn't really want to get out there and have to call somebody for a tow. Took a turn around the point, ran it a little, brought it back. Billy's good with engines."

"Sure he is," Moody says. He's looking at me, twisting the end of his mustache like a movie villain. I don't even think he knows he does it. “You know,” he says, “we chased somebody in a similar boat this morning.”

“I take it you didn’t catch him?”

“He got into the fog.”

“Pity,” I say.

Moody squints at me. “So we’re resorting to random checks.”

“Random,” Polky snorts from off to the side.

Moody takes a slow look at him, turns back to me. “Do you mind?”

“Knock yourself out.” I cut the engine, step out, and tie off the lines. Moody climbs aboard, slides the engine hatch off first thing and shines a beam of light in there. Polky grunts and turns a bucket over and sits down to have a smoke.

“Go ahead and take off,” I tell him. “I’ll entertain the troops.”

Polky stands up, but Dickless Tracy says, “He stays,” crosses her arms, and spreads her legs out like Superboy. She’s rugged for a girl, all pumped up like a lightweight lifter.

Polky gives out this big sigh and sits back down.

Officer Thibeault stares at him.

“Relax,” Polky says.

“Sir, please keep your comments to yourself,” she says. Polky half-grins at me, but I can tell he’s worried. Maybe he thinks they’ll find a trace of the warp somehow. When Moody bangs something below, Polky lifts an eyebrow. Finally Moody squeezes back into the wheelhouse, probes around there with the flashlight. Then he snaps the light off and climbs back over the rail onto the float.

“Well?” I say.

“She’s clean.”

“Did you check the bilge?” Polky says.

“Shut up, Polky.” Moody sticks a cigarette in his mouth, reaches into his shirt pocket for a wooden match, and snaps it with his thumbnail. The match flares and he lights his smoke. Then he shakes the match out and drops it over the side. “You really ought to stop hanging around with this piece of trash," he says, jerking a thumb at Polky. "It don't do you any good."

"That's what they tell me," I say.

Polky ducks his head. His hair falls down like a curtain around his face and he shakes his head slowly.

Moody says, "So where'd you dump it?"

"Dump what?" I say.

The little clam cop steps up and jabs a finger at my chest. "Listen, sir," she says. "We know what's going on here! I advise you to cooperate with us."

I just look at her.

Moody says, "Troy, you're no Polky, even if he's got you talked into something. I'll tell you what, you look me in the eye and tell me you didn't make a run." He looks *me* in the eye, and he's right, I can't lie to his face. I'm going to have to say something lame, and Moody will know for sure I was up to no good.

But then his partner says, "I doubt he's going to *confess* to anything!"

Moody keeps staring. "Relax, Officer Thibeault."

"I'm relaxed," she says. "But I can't believe we're not going to pat them down."

Moody keeps staring at me. I try to hold on.

"*I'll* pat them down," she says.

Moody sighs and turns. "Where's your probable cause?"

"I'll write the report."

"Nope," Moody says. "We don't do things that way."

Polky snorts, and both clam cops stare at him. Moody hooks his thumbs on his gun belt. Polky looks back from the tops of his eyes, which makes me nervous. You never know with Polky. But then he looks down and things ease up.

Moody turns back, says, "I still think you made a run." But he's not getting into it again, he knows it's over and he just waves a hand and heads toward the ladder. Thibeault and I follow. She kind of swaggers, with both thumbs in her gun belt, and keeps her eyes on me in a way that I find pretty goddamn annoying.

"So who sic-ed you on us?" I say when we get to the ladder.

"What makes you think that?" Moody says.

"You'd be home in bed otherwise."

Moody smiles, but Thibeault says, "Sir, I'd advise you not to jump to any conclusions."

"Thanks for the advice," I tell her.

She walks around in front of me, cap low on her forehead, knobby little chin stuck out like the last two inches of a baseball bat. She stares up at me and I stare right back: everybody seems to want to push me around lately and I'm getting a little tired of it.

"You seem to have a problem," she says.

"You think so?"

"Yes, sir, I think you have a problem with someone like me wearing a badge."

"No," I say. "I like a split-tail as well as anyone."

Thibeault's face burns red and her hand goes to her pistol. For a second I think she's going to gun me down right there. Polky can't smother a laugh, which doesn't help. But then Moody steps between us.

"That wasn't called for, Troy," he says.

"Sorry," I say.

Thibeault looks at him like she's waiting for more, and when it doesn't come she marches over to the ladder, yanks herself up the rungs, and swings over the top onto the wharf. We hear her boots on the planks as she stomps down the wharf toward the parking lot.

"Lucky you," I tell Moody.

"Never mind me," he says. He snaps his cigarette into the water and says, "Enough of this shit." He puts a foot up on the lowest rung, slaps a hand on the highest rung he can reach, and starts climbing with a grunt.

"Take it easy," I say.

"*You* take it easy," Moody says. He keeps climbing.

After Moody shuffles off, Polky says, "What about that little douche-bag?"

"She's something else," I say.

"And Moody talking about me like that!"

"The nerve," I say.

We walk over to the boat.

"So who do you think tipped them off?"

"I'm guessing Bobby Lawson." I free my lines and toss them one at a time into the boat, then step aboard and look back at Polky. I'm jittery now that it's over, but I try not to show it.

"Would he do that?" Polky says.

"If he thought he still owed me."

Polky steps back from the boat as I start the *Julie Marie*'s engine. We each raise a hand as I drift away from the float, then I crack the throttle open and turn to putt out through the soup. It's still thick as hell as I cross the harbor and when I'm even with the point I open her up. There's one last foggy stretch and then I'll be home. I'm shivering from the long night, from the clam cops, too, and I need coffee wicked. But since there's none on board, I crack the last lukewarm beer.

Steaming toward Pequot, I watch the drops of water converge on the windshield. The bay has gone sleepy under its fog quilt, and I keep an eye on the compass and think about the clam cops and Griffin and Bobby Lawson and Polky. I think about the Zeagull and Trace White and mortgages and lost parents and ex-wives. And Danny Brinker. And the TV people. Oh yeah, can't forget about them. They were a big part of this whole deal and they started showing up right after my meeting with the Zeagull.

SIX

I sat at the light, still steamed about Zeiglaar. A black Lincoln waited ahead of me. Several reasonable chances went by and the Lincoln didn't budge, so I settled in to wait, looking down the street at brick office buildings, the village green across from them, the frame buildings with picture windows at street level. It was a pretty town, I had to admit. But I liked it better when there were still bait shacks on the waterfront and a sawdusty old boat shop where we drifted down after school to hang out. There'd been a dozen working boats then, a hoist where the boardwalk now was, and traps stacked everywhere. We'd slouch around drinking coffee out of Styrofoam cups, bumming cigarettes from the lobster fishermen. It was a bit rough and tumble, the way *we* wanted to be, but then people moved in who couldn't understand why fishermen had to make all that noise so early in the morning. And they didn't like the smell of the bait shacks, or the language. When there were enough of them, they pushed through a noise ordinance. Then, a year or two later, you couldn't load bait. Then you couldn't work on your gear on town property. After a while they drove the last lobster-buyer out of town, and when that happened everybody pretty much had to follow him to Owls Head and set up shop there.

Finally the Lincoln crawled across the intersection and down to the five-way. It rolled straight through, and I turned down Ferry Street—only a block long—to the town landing. I nosed in against the boardwalk and looked out at the *Julie Marie* over in front of Brinker's. Polky's boat—*Lainey P,* named after *his* ex-wife—was there, too. They looked natural together, like a postcard. I got out of the pickup and walked up to Captain Cobb's.

Inside Cobb's, Danny Brinker was at the bar with his arms around a plate of chicken wings. Danny is some kind of a dwarf, but it's all in the legs. Sitting down, with his long back and big head, he was almost as tall as I was. Above him there were buoys, netting, and smiling plastic lobsters hanging off the ceiling. The windows were porthole-shaped. I sat down, snatched one of the chicken wings, and slurped the meat off the bone.

"Thanks for sharing," I said.

"Fucker." Danny Brinker said.

Molly Ring came over and said, "Look what the cat dragged in." She'd cut her hair off, dyed it bright yellow, and spiked it up with some kind of gunk. She'd been in the new tanning booth at the hairdresser's again from the looks of her skin, which was the color of an old moccasin. Molly was a local girl, ten years older than Danny and me.

I told her, "Nice 'do."

"Thanks, honey." She patted her hair and poured pints of beer for us. "There you go," she said, and wandered back down to the other end of the bar, walking on her toes like a dancer. I liked Molly. She was tough, good-looking, and didn't mind taking care of herself, either. Sometimes you'd see one of the young guys nursing his last drink while everybody else was leaving, and you pretty much knew what was going on with that.

"So what are you up to?" Danny said.

"Nothing much."

"How's the fishing?"

"Sucks," I told him.

"It'll pick up."

"I'm glad somebody thinks so."

I bought another order of wings and sat drinking with Danny until five o'clock, when the suits started coming in: lawyers, realtors, and bankers. Pequot was full of them lately and they all got off work at the same time. They made the place crowded and noisy, and when Niki Harjula walked in with another fashion-plate guy, I decided that was quite enough for one night.

I made a face at Danny and said, "I'm out of here."

"Wait up," Danny said. He hopped off the stool. On the way out Niki tried to wave me over, but I kept moving. Outside, we headed down Ferry Street, Danny taking three rocking steps for every two of mine. Past the boardwalk I could see the salt water and a dozen sailboats. The sun was low behind town, putting the harbor in shadow, and a little breeze had come up. Polky's boat was gone now—on some crooked mission, no doubt—which left the *Julie Marie* as the only working boat. We walked past the tall tourist schooner—*Madeleine B*—tied up next to the boardwalk. They'd stripped off her winter plastic-and-strapping—a sure sign of spring.

"Want to sit down?" Danny said.

"Sure." I looked at the nameplates on the benches. All the bigwigs in town were represented. They'd had to donate to get a plaque, and of course as soon as one of them ponied up, the rest had to. I found the Trace White bench and plopped down, thinking: How's the view, Trace old boy?

Danny hopped up next to me and offered a cigarette. I lit up as somebody's springer came clicking along the boardwalk. The dog looked us over and kept going on down to Erky Jura's wharf. He looked like a nice dog, and made me think of when I was a kid, how our springer—Sam—would jump into the creek and spook the shags. And how his big ears would still be damp at night when he climbed into bed and put his chin on my stomach.

I turned away so I could swallow and blink.

I'm such a pussy sometimes.

"Check it out," Danny said.

I looked out at a blue sailboat running under power past the island. It came in past the marina, long and low in the water, with a center cockpit and a tall bare mast, and made its way towing a rubber dinghy to a spot near the granite wall at the head of the cove.

"Nice, huh?" Danny had an eye for sailboats.

This tall guy reversed engine until the boat stopped in the water, then climbed out of the cockpit and leaned from the stern to gaff the mooring. When he missed he said, "Oh, *fuck!*" and climbed lower on a little chrome ladder. He finally hooked the buoy and dragged it close enough to attach the pendant. He climbed back onto the undercut stern and stood with his hands on his hips, looking at the stone-wall boundary of the marine park. Then he nodded to himself and hopped down into the cockpit.

Another motor started up close below, and the town's harbor-master—one-armed Freddie Linscott—headed out in his launch. He was halfway out when a willowy blonde woman appeared on the sailboat, carrying a little duffle bag. You could tell she was good-looking just from the way she moved, like she was all confident and happy with herself. Linscott idled his engine and called up, "You got permission to use that mooring?" He was only about a hundred yards away from the boardwalk so we heard him without any trouble.

The sailor stared down at him. "We certainly do."

"Okay, next question," Freddie said. "You going to keep her moored to the stern?" He squinted up at the sailor, his one arm stretched across the wheel. I could remember when he came home from Vietnam with his sleeve pinned up. I was five or six at the time. We're cousins of some kind—my mother was a Linscott—and we got pretty friendly once I was old enough not to be considered a *little kid*.

"Shouldn't I?" the man said to Linscott.

"Up to you. But if we get a blow, sometimes it comes in off the mountain and does funny things in here." He wagged his head toward the mountain behind town.

"Are you expecting a big blow?"

"You never know."

"We'll keep an eye on it," the sailor said. "I prefer working from the stern."

"Suit yourself." Freddie swung the launch around, looked up at Danny and me as he putted back to his slip. On the sailboat the man and the woman gathered their things and climbed down into the dinghy. The man fired up the outboard and ran them in. At the float he scrambled out and reached a hand down for the woman. At the top of the gangway the woman stopped and stretched. Her husband—I figured they were married—watched her pretty closely. He had a long pointy nose and a big mop of sandy hair, and he was wearing baggy white shorts and a fleece pullover with the collar turned up.

Danny whistled, too low for them to hear. "Money," he said.

"Gee," I said. "You think?"

They strolled along the boardwalk. The man had that rich-guy walk going: short steps, locked knees, chin up. They came up to the Trace White bench and the blonde woman gave us the once-over and said, "Hello," with a little shake of her head. She had a ski-jump nose and a small chin. One of those fox-shaped faces. Tiny crow's feet at the corners of her eyes. She looked at me with a little smile, as if I must like what I was seeing. I mean, she was *right* and all that. I checked her finger and, yep, there was a ring.

Her husband said, "Hello there."

Hello there is rude in my book, so I didn't answer.

But Danny said, "Howdy!"

The sailor looked right over Danny's head, nodding like he was happy with what he saw, but wasn't going to go overboard about it. "Lovely little town," he said.

"We like it," Danny said.

The sailor smiled. "We're with *American Road*. I imagine you've heard? We thought we'd sail up a little early. We're supposed to have lunch at a place called the Lord Pequot Inn. I wonder if you could point us in the right direction?" He was still rubbernecking, talking to Danny without looking at him.

"Up to Main Street, turn right. You can't miss it." Danny rummaged through his wallet until he found a business card. He held it out in his stubby fingers: "I've got the marina across the way. If I can help you out at all, you just let me know. I've got plenty of space, guys that can run around for you. I've got a generator if the power goes out. Ten thousand watt. You get a pretty good view of the town from there, too. You can borrow the dinghies to go back and forth." He talked fast, to get it all out before the man could move on.

"Well, thank you," the *American Road* man said. He put the card in his pocket and snaked an arm around his wife. He looked at me, then Danny. "Super," he said. He gave his wife a squeeze, and she smiled up at him. "Shall we?" he said.

His wife said, "Toodle-oo," and let her husband tow her away. They moved off across the parking lot toward the square, walking side by side around the corner onto Main Street, the guy talking into his wife's ear the whole time.

Danny lifted a hip, stuck his wallet away.

"Wipe your chin off," I told him.

"Hey, his money's as good as anybody else's."

I blew smoke out like I was disgusted, but I didn't really blame him. You had to do what you had to do. I heard toenails on wood and turned to watch the springer come back up the boardwalk from Erky's. I managed to reach out and ruffle the curly hair on his head before he trotted along to the wooden footbridge where the Pequot River came into the harbor. Off he went, clickety-clacking across the footbridge. Then Freddie Linscott came along the boardwalk, shaking his head. "Must be summer already," he said.

"Looking that way," I said.

He laughed and walked on, his one arm swinging.

"That girl was all tits and ass," Danny said when he was gone.

I tapped ash off my cigarette onto the boardwalk. "Did you ever see a rich guy with a homely girl?"

"Not lately."

"Not never."

"So get yourself some money." Danny grinned at me.

"Sure, I'll kiss ass like you."

"Join up with your buddy Polky."

"Don't tempt me," I said.

"You'd live better," Danny said, "'til you went to jail, anyways."

I snorted and looked out at the sailboat tied up at the stern. I shook my head. Then I did start thinking about Polky. Maybe I *ought* to join up with him, I thought, but I still wouldn't have said it was a real possibility if anyone had asked. I'd known Polky forever, and he was my pal, but there was no doubt he was headed for jail sooner or later. And I figured it might put a damper on any attempt to solve my problems if I was rotting in prison.

SEVEN

It had never occurred to me that it was a big deal, paying a week or two late to a *local bank*. But I realized now that counted for nothing, so for the next few days I went dawn to dusk, busting ass until my back was killing me and my bad knee was about to give. But the fishing was still lousy, so I hardly gained on the situation. It was even more of a waste because I couldn't properly enjoy the weather: calm water, lovely sunrises over The Havens and Big Branch, a soft breeze from the south that made it feel almost like summer. Normally I'd have been set up pretty well with those conditions that early in the season. But then that changed, too, just to make things ideal. The temperature dropped overnight, the dew point rose, and I was woken by foghorns. I stuck my head under the window shade, watched the Shag Island beacon glimmer in the soup, and thought, Great. But it was no huge surprise. Any fisherman knew that stuff never really went away, just moved back and forth in the gulf.

I dropped the shade, rolled out of bed, took a boiling-hot shower, and shuffled down to the kitchen, where I scarfed down a bowl of Cheerios, a glass of OJ, and a stale jelly donut. I stacked the breakfast dishes in the sink, feeling a little guilty, as if Julie Marie were still around to complain.

In the shed I stepped into my rubber boots and grabbed a hoodie off a nail in the wall. Outside I could hear the condensation dripping down through the leaves. When I got up onto Hull Street I could barely see the light at the corner through the swirling and shifting fog. I walked down the street, smelling the harbor, as if the heavy air was carrying a load of brine. At the stop sign I turned down Seaview Street, heading for the landing, where I'd left the *Julie Marie* yesterday, too lazy to row up the creek.

I walked downhill past homes with landscaped yards and stone walls. Some were old sea captains' houses with gables and widow's-walks and wrap-around porches; others were modern, with lots of glass and stone. They were all quiet: it was too early for anyone but a fisherman to be out, and there weren't but two of us left in Pequot. And one of these days, I thought, clumping down the hill, they'll catch Polky smuggling and throw his fat ass in jail, and then you'll be the last of the Mohicans, won't you?

I moved down-slope toward the square. It bummed me out how the rich people had taken over, even to the point of corrupting the town's name. We always pronounced it *Pee-kwot,* but they were slowly changing it over to something that sounded like *Pay-cot.* It made me want to gag when I heard them down at the landing—the *swanks*, as Polky called them—talking out of their goddamn beaks.

I looked downtown, where the mist hung around the buildings like a fine-gauge net, and before long I was picturing King Neptune wading out of the harbor, cinching that net, turning and dragging the whole damn town—the homes and tourist traps and church steeples; the grocery store and drugstore and condos—right back into the sea with him, leaving bare rock and grass, trees and brush.

We could start the hell over.

I walked onto Erky Jura's wharf. My boots were beginning to loosen up. At the end of the wharf I passed the schooner and clopped along the boardwalk to the gangway. It was low tide, and from the spotlight overhead I could see mud, rocks, mussels and seaweed, and a grocery cart some drunk must have sailed off the boardwalk. This was a sacrilege: you couldn't have trash like a grocery cart cluttering up *The Prettiest Harbor in Maine.*

I walked down the gangway to the float. It wasn't bad, this early in the morning. The dark and the fog covered up most of the town's *improvements.* I lit a cigarette, took five to enjoy it. But before I'd smoked it down the noise started up from Danny's. There was a truck, the generator, voices. I realized that it must be the TV people, getting things set up. I was surprised they started so early.

I swung on board the *Julie Marie* and stowed my ditty-bag in a corner of the wheelhouse. Then I stepped back onto the float and looked at my reflection in the glass porthole in the side of the cuddy. I'd forgotten to brush my hair after my shower, so it was sticking up and I combed it with my hands, though for no good reason: I would come back greasy and dirty no matter how I started out, and no one would say, "He stinks, but at least his hair's neat!" But I messed with my hair and looked at my image and wished I were more of a Hull instead of a Linscott: I loved my mother, but always wanted to look more like the old man, kind of dark and dangerous.

I jumped when somebody banged down the gangway, but as soon as I heard the "Hey, hey, hey," I relaxed again, knowing it was just Eddy Cranberry, coming by to lend a hand.

Speaking of stinky.

Eddy was a serious burnout whose real name was Laukka. He was strong as hell and a hard worker, but he didn't know enough to clean up afterwards, which made him a little hard to take sometimes. He liked to hang around the landing, guzzling from a plastic bottle of cranberry juice, and disrupting the flow of tourists like a big, smelly rock in the middle of a stream.

He did police the area, though. He'd decided at some point that it was one of his jobs. Another was helping me on the boat, which was no one's fault but my own: a while back there was an editorial in the weekly rag about *unsavory locals* and *their effect on the Pequot ambience,* and we all knew they were talking mostly about Eddy, so I started giving him some work, just to be contrary. Eddy decided we were partners then, and now, whenever he spotted the *Julie Marie,* he made a point of showing up and pitching in.

Eddy shuffled up in his overalls and flannel shirt, still mumbling, "Hey, hey," which is all he knew how to say since he'd scrambled his brains. But he was still no dumber than some of the sternmen I'd seen come down the pike, and if not for his smell he'd have been generally better company.

I set Eddy to cleaning the foredeck while I started in on the main deck. She was actually not too bad: I'd gotten a lot of it done running in the day before, with the saltwater hose. But you could always find something to do if you were stalling. I just wasn't that eager to go out and haul up empty traps in the pea soup. It sucked big time when you weren't making any money.

I thumbed a tight stream across the planks, washing starfish, crab shells, and bits of bait along to the scuppers, part of me appreciating how nicely the water beaded up on the deck.

Out in the gloom a foghorn let out a long hoot.

"Fuck you, too," I told it.

"Hey!" Eddy said. He had a thing about cussing. Sometimes I forgot.

"Sorry, buddy," I said.

He stared at me, then picked up the mop. I took the hose back and muscled it around the pegs; it was cold and didn't want to bend. I looked around at the fog and thought, Ah hell, who are you kidding? and I swung back aboard and tapped the fuel gauge, watching it settle at the quarter-tank mark. So I'd be gassing her up. More marks on the old tally sheet.

I heard a motor and looked up to see Danny Brinker coming out of the mist in an inflatable skiff. Danny putted past the tall side of the tourist schooner, looking up at the mast like he was checking for college girls. But it was a little early for that. It was wishful thinking, anyway. Polky had managed to nail one once, but he'd caught her drunk at Captain Cobb's, and when she'd sobered up she wouldn't have anything more to do with him, which broke poor Polky's heart for a day or two. He thought of himself as a college kid, too, because he'd graduated from the Maine Maritime Academy.

Danny drifted up, and I gave him a look before ducking down

into the cuddy. I lifted the V-bunk to grab a quart of motor oil and climbed back through the little door to the wheelhouse. I tipped the cover off the engine hatch, twisted the oil cap off, and poured in the oil. Then I replaced the cap on my thirty-thousand-dollar engine.

Brinker was standing on the float, wiping the fog off his face. He stuck the rag back in his hip pocket and wrinkled up his nose, looking at Eddy. But he didn't dare say anything.

"So you went and did it," I said, looking across at the bright lights. I swung onto the float, lifted the lid on the trash can, and dropped the oil container in.

Danny shrugged.

"How do they like the fog?" I said.

"Not too much," Danny said.

"Will it mess them up?"

"They don't know yet."

I spit out toward the marina. "So why'd they come here, anyway?" Usually they went to Bar Harbor, or Camden. Not Pequot.

Pay-cot.

"Old Hartley likes it up here," Danny said.

"I never saw him around."

"Well, he don't hang out at Cobb's," Danny said. "Hey, you're right in the line of fire, you know." He nodded in the direction of the marina. Pieces of it appeared and disappeared as the fog shifted around. "Why don't you hang a *Welcome to Pequot* off your boat, get yourself on TV?" he said.

"Why don't I hang a *Fuck You!* instead?"

Eddy dropped the mop and jumped down to the float. He put his hands on his hips, his face all screwed up to show how disgusted he was, the cords in his arms and neck standing out like twine. He was a little scary when he was pissed off—there was always the feeling he just might go lunatic—and I backed away a step.

Danny eased out of range, too.

I said, "Sorry, buddy, I forgot again."

But Eddy'd had it. He gave me his ugliest look and stuck out his hand. I dug into my pocket, found a five-dollar bill, and handed it over. Eddy made a fist around it, shoved the fist in the pocket of his overalls, and marched off up the gangway.

Hey, hey, hey, hey.

Danny grinned up at me. The float rocked underfoot and the big metal couplings that held the float to the pilings rattled. The tide was turning in, moving things. I yawned and looked around: couldn't see Burnt Mountain yet, but I could make out the rocky little waterfall where the Pequot River ran out into the harbor from under Main Street, and I could see the edge of the saltwater park at the head of the harbor, where the grass had already come in thick and green. It was a pretty town all right, grown up along the shape of the river valley. I liked the whole deal: the smell of low tide, and the seagulls squawking, and the floats rattling and clanking, and the foggy jumble of pilings under Danny's two long piers where the TV people were setting up.

Damn TV people.

I looked down at Danny, and he shrugged.

"That TV business won't help," I said.

"Nope." He looked toward his operation. Sunrise was coming and the fog brightened and swirled in even thicker. We couldn't see the lights or the piers any more across the way.

"Did they hire you too, or just your place?" I asked Danny.

"Oh, I'm gonna be doing this and that."

"Man," I said.

"If I didn't do it somebody else would. Erky Jura would take their money in a heartbeat." He nodded toward Erky's office at the end of the next wharf.

"Yeah, yeah," I said.

"Well," Danny said, "duty calls." He saluted and went hobbling up the gangway, using the pipe railings to haul himself along. I threw the lines into the boat and stepped aboard. I started the engine and threw the lever and the *Julie Marie* gurgled away from the float. My spirits lifted a little—I always loved setting forth. But when the channel brought me closer to Danny's marina I started thinking about Donald Hartley and his *American Road* show. I imagined people all over the USA listening to the broadcast, coming to town and falling in love with its *ambience*. I saw them talking to the asshole realtor who ran off with Julie Marie. Wouldn't that be ripe? The bank would have already repo-ed Hull Creek away from me. The nasty ponytailed realtor would take them up Hull Street and tell them what a lovely, private spot it was and how marvelous to have it so close to town. Of course the house wouldn't do, they'd have to raze it and build one of those glass and stone palaces.

I hocked something up and whistled it over the side, then I shoved the throttle forward. The *Julie Marie* surged ahead and I didn't look back until I was sure the sailboat had disappeared in the fog.

EIGHT

I ran out past the spruce island, watching for a particular long, fisty ledge that was always trying to rip a hole in my boat. It slid past just below the surface, and I swung back behind the wheel and checked the compass. My GPS sparked out a month before and I'd gone back to using the compass and the bottom finder. Which was no big deal: that's how everybody used to do it. But you had to be on your toes. I made along past Clam Cove, where Route 1 topped a bluff and, if it was clear and a little later in the day, I'd no doubt see RVs cruising along behind the guard-rails, like advance scouts for some bloody invasion. I hated RVs. It was an RV that hurt my parents, blowing a tire and skidding into their lane, turning their pickup into something that looked like one of the beer cans Polky liked to crush on his forehead. But I couldn't see the bluff this morning. My world had shrunk to a small circle of choppy water and mist, and I moved carefully in until I could hear surf on the granite breakwater. Then I pushed it across the outer harbor and around Owls Head Point and its beacon. I picked my way through sleepy boats and buoys into Owls Head harbor and up to Cormier's Pound, a tall covered wharf with wire fencing on both sides. I tied up at the float and climbed the clammy ladder to the wharf. There were seagulls standing on the roof, and when I waved my arms they lifted their wings and stepped around a little.

I found three tubs of herring with my name chalked on their sides, lowered them with the hoist to the float, dropped the gas hose, and climbed down to fuel her. Then I pulled myself back up the ladder and headed into the office, set back fifty feet from the edge of the wharf.

Inside, a pair of tourists was talking to Stan Cormier at his beat-up desk, and listening from the old, sprung couch by the Coke machine was none other than Bill Polky, looking like a pirate with his long hair and earring.

Polky winked at me and I headed over.

"Trying to find the lighthouse," he whispered.

This was a joke because last summer Stan had put a sign up in front of his wharf with directions to the lighthouse—just to cut down on those kinds of visits. It hadn't worked out that well, though. The tourists didn't seem to be able to trust the sign without verifying it inside.

Stan had his usual uniform on: jeans, t-shirt, and black leather vest, topped with a John Deere hat. He was jabbering, waving his hands, his big Adam's apple bouncing. The man and woman were nodding. They were in their mid-forties, dressed in khaki shirts and shorts with knee socks, and the man, for some reason, was wearing a hard-shell safari hat.

I looked at Polky. He shook his big head.

Stan stopped talking, lifted his cap to scratch his crew cut, and the tourists looked at each other and decided they could probably find the lighthouse now. Then the man asked Stan about the artificial cove rigged around the wharf, and Stan raised his hands and said, "It just keeps the lobsters from eck-scaping."

"Oh, is this a good lobster spot?"

Stan looked over at the couch. "It is once we fill it up," he said.

"You mean you *put* the lobsters in?"

"Well, how did you think they got there?"

"I thought perhaps they just lived there." The guy didn't seem to mind when Stan gave us another look. But then he noticed his wife smiling over at Polky and me, and he cleared his throat. She broke off looking at us and reached up to tap his safari hat with her wedding ring.

"Anyways," Stan said, "they don't live here."

The man nodded like he was filing it away. "Well," he said, "thank you so much for the information. We love it up here." He put an arm around his wife. "We're thinking of *buying* here, in fact. I certainly hope we haven't been an annoyance to you."

"Yes, thank you *so* much," his wife said.

"Don't worry about it," Stan said.

The woman looked over toward the couch again. I half expected her to come over and ask us to say something in our quaint Maine accents. But her husband turned her the other way and started her toward the door. They pulled the door shut, and I heard her say, "My goodness gracious!" as they left.

Polky gave out this belly laugh. "You see her drooling at Troy?" he said to Stan.

Stan laughed and looked sideways at me.

"Right now she's telling hubby how *stunning* he is," Polky said.

"Oh, here we go," I said.

Polky slapped his knee and rocked on the sofa. He'd been looking for chances to call me *stunning* since last summer. No matter that it wasn't anything I brought on myself, it still made good ammunition, and I knew at the time that I'd never hear the end of it. But I couldn't deny it had happened.

It had been a busy night and we were crammed into a little space at the stand-up end of the bar at Cobb's, drinking shots and beers, and these two women just sort of appeared out of the crowd. And one of them said, "Turn around," just like that.

At first I didn't even known she was talking to me. But then she tapped me on the shoulder and said, "Young man? Turn around," and when I did, she said, "Didn't I tell you he was *stunning?* All husky and sunburned, like a *Viking!*"

Her eyes were bloodshot and her face was red. She was probably in her mid-forties. Her friend was a little younger, with a ponytail that stuck out like a rooster tail through her Red Sox cap.

"Are you a lobster-man?" the friend said. "We're with the teachers' convention, see?" She grabbed the bottom of her t-shirt and pulled it down so I could read: *Teachers do it with class!*

"What's your name, anyway?" the first one said.

I turned away, a little sick to my stomach. I wasn't even all that good-looking, just fairly rugged, and I had blond hair, which tricked some people into thinking I was. Anyway, I turned my back on the teachers, hoping they'd leave. But Polky had been listening, and he leaned out and said, "He's a *lobster*man, all right. His name's Troy. *Troy the Viking,* we call him."

"Shut up, Polky," I said.

"Are you his friend?" the teacher said to Polky.

"I'm his best pal!" Polky said, and he scratched his nose so she could see where he was missing two fingers on his left hand. He claimed it was from a chainsaw accident, but I'd heard that he'd had a run-in with some local *businessmen* he'd been dealing with, whose noses were out of joint because he'd attempted to step out on his own, and that they'd used a pair of wire cutters to show him the error of his ways. Whatever it was, he'd turned up with a big bandage around his hand, and afterward a claw that he got pretty fond of and liked to wave around. Now he waved it toward the older teacher and wiggled the three fingers. The teacher stopped grinning and he said, "What's the matter, don't you think I'm *stunning*, too?"

The teacher looked over at her friend.

Polky turned his claw this way and that. "You know what?" he said. "With this thing here I could pick you up like a BOWLING BALL." He tapped the three fingertips together, and the teacher sort of pulled her head back and swallowed. Finally her friend took her by the arm and led her back into the crowd. Then Polky sat back and grinned at me. "I guess that didn't appeal to them, huh?" he said.

"I'd say not."

"Maybe if I was a great big stunning lobster-man." Polky tipped his head back and laughed, and he'd been laughing about it ever since. Now he slapped his knee again and giggled. Stan shook his head, but he had a shit-eating grin, too. I ignored both of them and walked over to the desk to check my balance. I grabbed Stan's records book and ran a finger down the column under my name. "Jesus Christ," I said.

"Nobody else is catching any either," Stan said.

"Big Branch," Polky said between chuckles.

"Fat lot of good that does me," I said. They always caught more at Big Branch Island. It was a closed grounds, though, like most areas were. Sometimes a man would die with no kid to take over and a fringe family would move in, but otherwise not much changed. After my old man died, I came home to find a bunch of Lawsons setting traps in Hull territory, and I tried warning them off with a half-hitch around the spindle of a buoy, then, when that didn't work, a few buoys lashed together. But I finally had to corner Bobby Lawson at the pound and knock him around. Afterward the Lawson tribe went back to clam-digging.

I thumped the records book shut.

Polky cleared his throat, and when I looked over, he nodded toward the door. Then he said, "See ya," to Stan, got up, and left. After a minute or two, I followed.

Outside it was gloomy, the wharf damp and slippery.

I put a foot up on the end beam.

Polky lit a cigarette, snapped his Zippo shut, and blew smoke out into the fog. "So what do you think, Viking-boy?" he said.

"I think you're an asshole," I said.

Polky grinned. "So, I was wondering," he said.

"What?"

"If you might be up for a warp run."

I looked at him. "Isn't that kind of small potatoes for you?"

"Not necessarily," Polky said. "Perfect night for it."

"Tonight?"

"*Yeah*, tonight."

I guess this was where it all really started, the slippery slope and all that. Normally I would have said, "Thanks but no thanks,"—my usual response to Polky's bright ideas. But I was in a different place after my little meeting with the Zeagull. So I jokingly said, "Whose boat?"

Polky grinned. "Oh," he said, "I ain't had a ride in yours yet, have I?"

"My GPS is out," I told him.

"You need GPS to find Nova Scotia?"

"I might."

He just snorted, and I looked out at the fog and considered. Things had changed for the worse, and I'd been worried to begin with. And it wasn't that enormous a crime, smuggling duty-free rope. It wasn't like bringing drugs in, say. I lit up a cigarette and looked back at Polky, who was still grinning, like he knew my answer ahead of time. I shrugged my shoulders. "What the hell," I said.

"Sweet!" Polky held up a hand.

I ignored it. I don't ever high-five anyone, and Polky knew that, but he always held his hand up anyway so he could laugh at me for being stubborn. We went back into the office and I waited by the door while he thumbed quarters into the Coke machine. He pressed the button just as Danny Brinker hobbled in.

"Hey," Danny said to us.

"Well, well," Polky said. "Look who's out slumming."

"Picking up some lobsters for the man," Danny said, putting his hands on his hips. He was a head shorter than everyone else and wearing this green and white rugby shirt he'd cut the sleeves off. One thing about Danny: he had a rich-boy face, little snub nose and blue eyes and this silky gold hair. He looked like a god from the neck up, and you knew he would have had it made if only he'd had a normal body. Sometimes I thought that must have driven him crazy.

"Old Hartley like his critters, does he?" Polky asked.

"Oh, he's a bear for 'em," Danny said.

"I'd like to see him with one of them little plastic bibs on." Polky let himself down onto the sofa and took a slug from the can of Coke.

"Well, he don't wear the bibs," Danny said.

"I'll bet he does."

"Naw, he's past all that."

"So how's he to work for?" Polky had his innocent face on now.

Danny squinted at him. "His money's fine."

Polky grinned. "How do you like him when he's reaming you out in public?"

"Don't believe everything you hear."

"What'd you do, forget to swallow?"

"Fuck you, Bill!" Danny said.

Polky rocked forward on the sofa, laughing. "I'm just shitting you!" he said. "Hey, is it all right to come and watch?"

"People do," Danny said, a little stiffly.

"Maybe I'll drop in."

"See you guys later," I said then. I had to get moving if I was going to get back in time to go across. And I guessed I was going to do it. The funny feeling had gone away pretty quick. I guess I'm adaptable that way.

Polky got up to follow me. Outside in the soup I said, "I should be done by four or so."

"Want me to pick up some beer?"

"You might."

"I'll stop by the Pik Kwik."

We looked around when Stan and Danny came out of the office. Stan had hip boots on and carried a long-handled net. Danny had the red-and-white lobster-pack. He looked back at us as they walked through the roofed part of the wharf. They went out of sight but we could still hear his quick, scuffy steps beside Stan's slower ones.

"Well, I'll see you," I told Polky.

He saluted with his claw and walked off.

I started down the ladder, hoping there wasn't some fool running blind in the bay. It was a little early for that, but you couldn't depend on the summer season any more. At one time is was between

Memorial Day and Labor Day, but lately it was stretching in both directions and you never knew when some flatlander with more money than brains might decide he was a real, full-weather *mariner.*

I wrestled the bait tubs into the boat, in a hurry now, so I could head off for the Maritimes and make a little money. It was kind of exciting to think about. A little worrisome, too. But at least it was different. At least I would be doing something besides running out and hauling empty traps.

NINE

I watched the bottom finder and compass until I ran up on my first set of buoys, and then I gave the wheel a yank and leaned over the side with the gaff. I snapped the line over the snatch block, took a turn around the hauler, and in a few seconds the first trap appeared below, distorted and rising fast. It burst to the surface, and I hauled it aboard and slid it along the rail, then did the same for its mate. I ran doubles here because the bottom was too rough for trawls. I dug through both traps and found nothing but whore eggs—sea urchins—and starfish.

I flipped the urchins over the side, sailed the starfish like little Frisbees. I rebaited the traps, locked them shut, and shoved them overboard, watching the line slither after them, then the maroon-and-white buoys.

The next set had two undersized lobsters, and I picked them up and thought for a second about lunch. You put them in a pot of seawater and cook them right on the engine block. But then I tossed them over the side. I'd already decided to commit one crime today and that was probably enough. I moved on, running up to the buoys, hauling the traps, pulling out the critters, measuring the close ones, banding the keepers, and dropping them into the salt water well just aft of the wheelhouse. I bagged the bait, stuck the bags into the traps. Every now and then I noticed how rank the bait was. You forgot that, and then you went ashore and people avoided you like you were Eddy Cranberry.

I steamed through the fog, worked another empty set, threw the traps over, and goosed it. It was pretty damn discouraging. Old-timers said it was the late spring—the water was still too cold for the critters to move around. But maybe it was just a down cycle. Whatever it was, I knew if I didn't do better I was going to be back in The Zeagull's office.

I leaned over the rail with the gaff.

By 11:00 the fog had moved back past the islands and it was warm enough to peel off a couple of layers of clothes. I sat on a tote in my t-shirt and slicker pants, working on a PB&J sandwich, drifting near a string of traps marked by buoys at either end. I'd recently jigged them onto mud bottom here and could run trawls. I heard another boat working off to the south, its engine going loud and quiet as it turned toward me then away. I poured coffee, put the cap back on the silver thermos. I'd hung my rubber gloves inside-out next to the engine stack, where they might not dry all the way but would at least be warm when I put them back on. I sipped coffee and looked down the bay at the fogbank. It was a grimy color, like somebody had smeared it onto the horizon with a dirty thumb. There was yellow in it, brown too if you looked close. I took a bite of my sandwich and watched the fog while I chewed. When I was done with lunch I started right in hauling again, the work going faster now that I could see, but my elbow was burning and an ache had worked up my back and into my neck. I wished for the thousandth time that I could afford a sternman.

I worked as fast as I could, but was still fifty traps shy of my goal of two hundred when the fogbank moved in past the islands and headed my way. It was tall and thick and the whole width of the bay, and it was moving fast. I was soon running blind again. I pulled my sweatshirt on and spun the wheel to head in. Screw the rest of them, I thought. It would be one thing if they were packed.

I kept an eye on the depth finder, pictured the landscape down there, the animal life, vegetation, mountains, canyons, schools of fish like flocks of birds. I ran in, listening to some other fisherman on the VHF talking to his wife. After a while I shut the radio off. It was thick-of-fog when I eased back in to the pound. Bill Polky was sitting on the beam with his boots hanging down and a case of PBR at his elbow. The Breakfast of Champions, he called it.

"Any luck?" he said.

"Oh yeah," I told him. "I can hardly stand it."

Polky lowered the hoist and I sent the totes up. He looked them over and said, "This ain't gonna make it, Troy-boy."

"No shit," I said. I dumped the scraps over the side and climbed up with the empty tubs. I shoved them under the lean-to and looked back at Polky leaning on the hoist. "I'll be right out," I told him. He nodded and sat down. He lit up a smoke, hands cupped in front of his face.

"Quarter-pound a trap." I shook my head, stuck the money in my wallet, and stuffed the wallet away. Stan helped carry the totes out and dump them into the artificial cove. The water bubbled from three places on each side of the wharf.

"Everybody's complaining," Stan said on the way back.

"I never saw it so bad," I said.

"It's always bad in the spring, though."

"Last fall was the killer." Fall was when you made your stake, usually. But last fall had been ridiculous. Then the late spring had finished the job. I thought it was pretty amazing how close to the edge you could be without knowing it. A couple of years ago I'd had a new boat, a happy wife, money in my pocket.

I shook my head, walking beside Stan. We went into the covered section of the wharf and up to the office and he flicked a piece of paint off the window frame. He claimed he was going to break down and scrape the place and paint it one of these days. But he also said the lobsters didn't care, neither did the fishermen, so for now he worked at it one flake at a time. The wood was gray and damp where the paint peeled off.

Stan turned into his office and I walked through to the other side. Down on the float Polky was still sitting with the case of beer at his feet. "You ready?" I said.

"Born ready."

"I'll send down the hose. Top her off for me, will you?"

Polky spun the cap off the fuel pipe. He jammed the gun in and pulled the trigger. When he was done he sent the hose back and I wrote my total on the clipboard hanging off the pump. I climbed down the ladder. There didn't seem to be anybody around, but just in case, Polky ducked into the cuddy. I started the engine and worked us away from Stan's. We ran out between the Head and Monroe Island and when we reached the lighthouse Polky squeezed back topside. He was barely settled when we passed a dory coming the other way, close enough that even in the fog I could make out stacked hods and somebody that looked an awful lot like Bobby Lawson, sitting aft with his hand on the throttle. Bobby stared over but didn't nod or wave as he rode past, bobbing over our wake and disappearing.

"Oopsie," Polky said when he was gone.

I just shrugged. We could have been going home, for all Bobby knew. We headed off through the soup, crossing the bay in the direction of Deer Isle, and an hour later we were streaming up the coast. It was three or four hours to New Brunswick, then southeast across the Bay of Fundy, toward Nova Scotia, which sits like a huge foot pointing out to sea, connected to New Brunswick by its ankle. We were aiming for the heel. It was a pretty big trip, and we could feel the water get wider, the swells longer. The *Julie Marie* started to feel pretty small, especially in the fog where we couldn't see lights anywhere.

"We might be in it the whole way," Polky said.

"That wouldn't be bad."

"Nope." Polky tore a beer from the case, popped the top, and handed it over. I shifted on my feet and took a sip. He popped one for himself, tipped it up. Then he sat down on the engine hatch. We didn't talk much at first. It was a long trip to start gabbing right off the bat. I was antsy, too, still uncomfortable about this deal. But there was no turning back now. I nudged the wheel, let my thoughts drift as we steamed along through the dark. They eventually found their way to Julie Marie, which was no big surprise. I still missed her a lot, even though by the time she'd left I'd had it with the bedtime games. She'd been real good at making sure nothing happened, and then blaming me for it, and even though I knew what was going on, it was troublesome. But that didn't change the fact that we'd been together almost since she'd moved to town in the eighth grade. She was shy back then, and I'd always been wicked shy around girls, and we ended up together at a dance after a teacher put us together, and that was how it started. We kept it going all through high school and visited back and forth after I went to UMaine, and we got married when I came home to work the grounds.

She was still the only one I'd ever slept with.

I remembered how Julie would grab my thumb in one hand, my little finger with the other, and pull herself close to kiss me. That was before things started to go bad, of course. I was still amazed at how fast *that* had happened. One summer, fall, and winter, pretty much. It was after she'd taken the job at the realty. That was the beginning of the end. The realtors infected her with ideas about selling Hull Creek, and she thought that would solve all our problems. When I wouldn't go along she found another way to change things.

"What the hell," I said to myself.

"What's that?" Polky said.

"Nothing," I told him. Neither of us said anything more until we were halfway to Canada and Polky started in about me being a bad ass in training. Which I guess I was.

TEN

The Shag Island beacon brings me back to the moment, and I finish the lukewarm beer and drop the empty into the box by my feet. I steer past the island and Danny's marina, close enough to see barnacles on the pilings under the spotlight, and I have to pay attention. At my mooring, I cut the engine and climb forward to gaff the slimy line and switch the skiff out. I wipe my hands on my jeans, walk the skiff back, and swing down into the wheelhouse. I stow my gear and step into the tippy little craft, then push off and turn to dig with the oars. It's so quiet I can hear the skiff hissing through the water. But that only lasts until I'm halfway across, and then the marina wakes up. A diesel starts, a man shouts, a generator rattles on. Lights flash in the fog. I make my way under the bridge, putting my back into it against the current. I yank the oars hard, inch along to smooth water, then move around the bend and up the creek. The shags aren't up yet, but after my little excursion with Polky I probably don't deserve any applause this morning anyway. I watch my old house slide away and then I look over my shoulder and skim up to the end of the dock. It'll be sunrise soon, and the fog is starting to brighten and move around.

In the kitchen I look at my mother's old electric range, but I'm too tired to cook, so I go back outside, climb into the pickup, and back out of the driveway. I go down to the five-way and double back through downtown. Once I'm on the move it's better. Main Street is sound asleep, except for Scottie Lappinen's bakery. I roll down my window to smell the bread baking and my stomach lets out a rumble.

It's five miles to Rockland, a town as much about fishing and townies as Pequot is about rich people and tourists. There's a Coast Guard base and even an old fish-processing plant on a wharf. They have a motto, too, but it's not on a sign anywhere: *Pequot By The Sea, Rockland By The Smell.*

I drive through town and park in front of Gary's Lunch, a beat-up joint that's the only early breakfast dive left in the area. It's empty inside except for the old hawk-nosed town cabbie sitting by the window. He nods, his big nose disappears into the coffee cup and then he lowers the cup to the table and looks out the window. There's a cigarette in his other hand, and the smoke wanders up to the ceiling and hangs there.

I see Gary through the order window, wearing his dirty whites, slapping a green plastic plate down on the sill and yelling out, "Sand-ay!" He's a skinny guy who works with a cigarette in his mouth. As I watch, the ash falls onto the grill and he scrapes it out of the way with the side of his fork, then goes back to pushing the bacon around.

Sandy takes the plate over to the cabbie.

I look out the window, but you can't see anything for the fog. I drink my coffee and think about Julie Marie wanting to move down this way and wonder if I should have just gone along. Maybe I should have faced up to Pequot being a rich-folks town.

"To hell with that," I say to myself.

I'm dog-tired. When my eggs and bacon come I shovel them in and drink three cups of coffee. That helps a little, but I wish the cups weren't so shallow. I have a biscuit with raspberry jam and butter. I push the plate away and fire up a smoke when one of the Blandford boys slides onto the stool beside me, picks up my water glass, and sets it back down on some folded money.

"That was quick," I say.

"Ran into Polky." Blandford tips his John Deere cap and clumps back out the door in his rubber boots. Within a half hour three more guys have paid me for the warp they fished out of the cove. Then Stewie Lapinen shows up, an old friend of my father's. He's still a big man, but kind of gimped up these days. His nose looks like a bee stung it, and he wears big thick glasses now, but he's still fishing. He pokes around in his pockets, finds his cash, and hands it over.

"Like old times," he says, "paying a Hull for warp."

"Oh yeah?" I say.

"Christ, yes!" he says, and winks.

Sandy splashes coffee into our cups and pretends not to notice the money on the counter. On her way back to the kitchen she has to swerve around the Ingraham twins, who've come off the street to stand side by side inside the front door. When they come over I say, "Howdy, boys," and Ira Ingraham sticks out his hand and says, "Warp."

It sounds like *wop*.

I take his fishy wad of bills and stick it in my pocket without counting it, even though I'm probably being short-changed. The Ingrahams are throwbacks, and I don't want to mess with them. Polky's the only one I know who ever took one on, and after they went at it for a few minutes on the grass behind Captain Cobb's, Polky held up his hands and walked off. It shocked me to see him quit, but he told me later that it just wasn't any good: "You hit them," he said, "and unless you break something important, the sons of whores don't even feel it! And if you *did* happen to whip one of them, you'd only have to fight the other! Who needs that shit?"

I thank the Ingrahams, and they grunt and turn around to leave. It takes them a second at the door to decide who will go first. The door shuts and Stewie Lapinen shakes his head and goes back to his coffee. But then Bill Polky shows up, and Stewie says, "Christ!" as if seeing him is the last straw. He gets up, tugs his belt up on his shanks, and throws money on the counter for Sandy.

"Don't rise," Polky says as he comes up.

Stewie just heads for the door.

Polky turns to watch, then takes his chair. "He don't much approve of me, do he?" he says.

"Who does?" I say.

"Good point," Polky says. "HEY SANDY! How about some coffee for this weary pilgrim!" He runs both hands through his hair, sticking his chin out at her and grinning.

Sandy comes over and pours.

"Thanks, darlin'," Polky says.

"You're welcome, Billy."

"What are we doing tonight, sweetheart?"

"*I'm* going home to my husband."

"All right," Polky says. "Be that way."

Sandy walks off, moving her hips a little. Polky drums his fingers, plays with one of the zippers on his black leather jacket, jigs his feet on the floor. He's never been able to sit still. He looks around the room—it's just us and the cabbie, who's deaf as a hake—and smiles back at me. He looks fresh and awake. You'd never know he hasn't had any sleep, either.

"What?" I say.

He grabs my hand and slaps a roll of bills into it—a pretty thick slug of cash. I close my fist around it as Sandy comes over with the coffee pot.

"What the hell is this?" I say when Sandy's gone.

"Windfall profit, just like the oil companies."

"From what?" I say.

Polky just grins.

Then I remember how he patted himself down when he woke up on the *Julie Marie*. I remember a few other things, too, like the way he went up to see Griffin alone. I say, "Son of a bitch," and try to stuff the money into his jacket pocket. But Polky fends me off. His fingers feel like talons around my wrist.

"Keep it, you need it," he says.

"I don't like you using me that way."

"I didn't plan it."

"Bullshit."

Polky shoves my hand away and keeps his voice low. "You just hang onto that until I can explain," he says. "What happened was Griffy talked me into it. I was only after warp, swear to God." He looks over toward Gary, but Gary's paying us no mind at all.

I shift the money and dry my palm on my knee.

"I always go up to see Griffy alone at first," Polky says. "It's best that way. Last night he told me he needed to get a little product to someone, out of the blue. Hell, I just figured it was somebody upstairs looking out for you, since you need the money and I'd give you half."

"Not without telling me," I say.

"You'd make a fuss and screw everything up and then Griffy wouldn't trust me no more."

"So what was it?" I ask him.

"Just a little weed."

I give him a look: there's too much money for that.

"Soaked in something or other." Polky says. "But basically just weed."

"How much of it?"

"Couple pounds."

"Where'd you hide a couple pounds?"

"I got these pockets sewn in. Listen, think of it as an advance. For when you smarten up."

I'm still looking for a chance to stuff the cash back into Polky's pocket, but he's ready for me. "You were already breaking the law, Troy-boy," he says.

"There's a difference," I say.

"Like what?"

"Rope's not going to hurt anybody."

"Who am I hurting? Nobody's hanging around the schools, trying to get the third graders stoned. You know who buys it? Hippies that go to the Common Ground Fair. Dumb-ass dishwashers at the *Paycot* Resort. Regular guys who like to get a buzz on and get laid. Cancer patients, too, that can't buy it legal."

"What about the burn-outs like Eddy Laukka?"

"He didn't get that way from smoking pot."

"It's all part of the same deal," I say.

"Not with me it ain't. Not for the most part. Listen, Troy, you keep that. Go make a payment. Then think about throwing in with me and paying the whole goddamn thing off. I could use a little help."

I take a sip of my cooled-off coffee. Trying to get him to take the money back is a losing battle. And the trip's over and done with, so I decide I might as well keep it. But I do manage to say, "I'm not doing it again."

Polky just grins at me.

I shove the cash into my pocket. "And it's a loan," I say.

"Call it whatever you like," Polky says.

I look around. The cabbie's busy with his food. Sandy is talking to Gary in the kitchen; he's staring down at her like he doesn't believe a word she says. Nobody's paying us any attention.

Polky swings off his chair and leans up close to me. "Listen," he says, "You're like me. You're a Maine boy. Fucking swanks think they own the world, but they don't own you and me." He slaps me on the back. "I think I'll go check out the TV folks. Want to come?"

"I'm going home to bed."

"You big pussy," he says.

Sandy brings the check over, and Polky bows, sweeping his hand like it holds a fancy plumed hat. "Put it on Troy-boy's bill, darlin'!" he says. Then he leaves, slamming the door behind him. Sandy puts the slip on top of mine, walks to the cabbie to take his plate away, and heads for the kitchen. I pry a few of the Ingrahams' fishy bills loose and set them down with my slips.

Sandy comes back out of the kitchen and walks over.

"Keep the change," I say.

She holds the money in her thumb and forefinger and makes a face. I laugh and head outside. It's brighter, but still foggy. I climb into my pickup and drive back to Pequot. Other cars and trucks are starting to show up now, people going to work. Everybody's taking their time. It's fifteen minutes to get back to Hull Creek, and I barely have enough energy left to crawl into bed.

ELEVEN

It's the trip back from Nova Scotia and the Marine Patrol is chasing me around in fog that's so thick I have to shove through it to move around in the wheelhouse. Behind me there are bundles of warp scattered around the deck. Polky's not along on this trip, but I know he's waiting for me at the canal. I'm supposed to bring the stuff in so we can hide it under the bushes there. We're both kids, too, but I still have my new boat. The Marine Patrol is a mile astern with a huge spotlight trying to pick me out of the soup, and I'm anxious to unload, but I can't get at it. Then a storm comes up and throws the boat around, knocking me flat on the deck. The wind is howling, rain coming down in volleys, and I'm crawling across the deck, pulling myself up to the wheel, and hanging on for dear life. Meanwhile the clam cops are closing in, their own boat having no trouble at all in the wind and waves. I think that's pretty damn unfair, but what can I do about it? Then I hear Dickless Tracy over their loudspeaker, calling for me to come about and surrender. The storm picks up, building a sea under the *Julie Marie* so high that when I nose over, her ass end comes completely out of the water and the prop sings in the air. She teeters and falls, dropping fast toward the bottom. Then she starts coming apart: planks splinter and glass breaks, sparks shoot out of the console, the boat disintegrates until it's just me, the wheel in my hands and the prop behind me taking the big plunge. Just as I hit bottom, I snap upright in the bed, sweaty and confused. I see the clock radio on the windowsill, and it's two o'clock. I stare at it for a second and realize I've been sleeping. But I can still hear a prop revving, and that keeps me confused until I figure out that it's an engine taching up for real somewhere close. I tug the shade and let it flap up. Then I open the window. The fog is gone and the sun shines through the treetops. The noise comes from down the street. I roll out of bed, take a shower as hot as I can stand it. I towel off and put on clean skivvies, jeans, t-shirt, and socks. I feel a nervous relief that I'm not about to die and have my lobster-eaten body pulled out of the bay by the goddamn clam cops. I take my wallet, the warp money, my jackknife, and lighter off the night-stand and stick them in my pockets. Then I walk downstairs and out the side door. It's quiet on the creek, all the big birds spooked off, but when the noise from down the street pauses I can hear little birds everywhere, and off in the bushes a chipmunk raising hell about one thing or other.

I drive down to the corner and see Charlie Hamalainen's house bashed and broken, like it's been hit by artillery. A three-quarter-size dozer is backing away from the house. There's a *Demmons Construction* sign stuck into the lawn next to the driveway, and Brad Demmons himself is working the dozer, laying a wide double track in the lawn. He drives straight into the front wall and the dozer jumps forward as the wall collapses and dust billows from the house. Black smoke pours out of the dozer's stack. Brad looks over and raises a hand, and I wave back, then turn onto Seaview. I drift down past the yacht club, where somebody is standing on a step-ladder painting the eaves. I pry my way through the intersection and head south to the shopping plaza. I park and walk across the lot through sunlight slanting over the trees behind the town. In the bank three tellers are working. One of them, a chubby woman wearing those big glasses with the temples at the bottom, nods at me and says, "May I help you, sir?"

"I'll wait for Niki," I tell her.

Niki looks past her customer's shoulder and smiles at me.

The first teller frowns and says, "Next, then?" and a grim-looking businesswoman squeezes past me and rat-a-tats up to her window. Then Niki's customer leaves and I go on up.

"Back so soon?" she says.

I count out eleven hundred dollars and change, tear a pay coupon out of the pay book and fill in the blanks with the bank's chained-off pen. "Yep," I say.

"Why wouldn't you talk to me in Cobb's?" Niki says.

"I had to get going," I say, and slide the form over.

"It was who I was with, wasn't it?"

"It's none of my business who you're with."

"We were just talking," Niki says.

"Like I said, none of my business."

"If you say so." She scoops the money out of the way and reaches for a jar on her counter. There's a picture of a sad little girl in a torn dress on the label. Niki rattles the change in the bottle and says, "Since you're apparently loaded."

"Hell, she ought to be donating to me."

Niki just shakes the jar again.

I fold a ten-dollar bill until it fits into the slot.

"Don't you feel better now?" Niki says.

"No."

"Liar." She puts my money away and runs a receipt through some kind of automatic typer, then stamps the receipt and hands it over. She smiles at me and I remember when she treated herself to some dental work a couple of years back. They did a good job. At one time her teeth looked pretty bad.

"Thank you, ma'am," I say.

"I'm not a *ma'am*."

"Thank you, Ms. Harjula, then."

"I'm no *Mizz* either."

Then I hear Keith Zeiglaar's office door open, and he comes out and looks at me. I turn back to Niki and say, "I'm out of here."

"Okay, I'll see you later."

"Yes ma'am," I say.

"Troy!"

Back up the hill I turn off Seaview, coast into Charlie Hamalainen's driveway, and tap the horn. Brad Demmons squints over at me, looks at his watch, and switches off the dozer. All at once it's so quiet my ears ring.

"Sorry about the racket," Brad says when I walk up.

"What's going on?"

"Oh, knocking it down."

"I can see that much."

"You knew the bank got it back."

I nod and look at the caved-in house, at the splintered studs, plaster, drop-ceiling tiles on the ground. There's a lot to a house, once you start tearing it apart. More than you'd think.

"Guess they wanted the view, not the house." Brad looks at me with one eye closed.

"That was a good solid place," I say.

"Tell me about it."

"Some nice cabinet work, too."

"Yeah, I helped put them in."

"You'd think they'd give it away or something."

Brad sticks two fingers into his shirt pocket and pulls out a pack of Salems. He offers me one. I shake my head—can't abide menthol—and he lights up and sits back, crossing his arms, smoking without using his hands. "You give it away," he says, "and you have to deal with the riff-raff. It's inconvenient, see? This way it's over and done with." He looks at something on the other side of the street, down in the harbor, and when I turn around I see Danny Brinker bringing a group across in an inflatable. Danny takes his cap off, dunks his other hand in the water and runs it through his hair like he's combing it. Then he puts the cap back on.

I look back at Demmons. "They got somebody lined up to buy it?"

"I don't know. Most likely."

We look at what's left of the house until Brad finishes his smoke. Then he raises his eyebrows and reaches for the ignition key. I step back and he fires the dozer up and drives across the lawn into a corner post of the house, which starts another wall falling. When it's down I can see the honeysuckle bush Charlie put in for the birds. Past the bush, the creek sparkles in the sunlight. I back away, over to the pickup, wondering who my new neighbor will be. Some *swank*, no doubt. Some rich puke. Maybe I'll bake him a fucking casserole.

I sit in the wicker rocker on the deck, listening to the dozer. I hear dump trucks, too, gears clanking, tailgates rattling. I go inside for a beer, then back out to the deck. After an hour or so and another beer the noise stops. Then the big birds come back and I have a couple more beers, watching the fish hawks. They look way too heavy for their twig perches. As I watch, one of them tucks his wings and dives into the water. He surfaces with a fish, shivers the water off his feathers, and flies away. Seagulls try to pester him into dropping his catch, but without any luck. The osprey disappears over the trees.

I watch the show until the sun drops behind the trees and shadows grow along the creek to the bridge. When the harbor is completely shaded, the fog starts back in off the bay, and pretty soon the harbor disappears. Then the fog rolls up the creek like something out of *The Twilight Zone* and the foghorns honk like giant, sad geese. I hobble down the steps, stiff from sitting, and limp down Hull Street for one more look at Charlie's. The house didn't put up much of a struggle, no matter how well it was put together. I wander around, finishing my beer and drop-kicking the empty onto the house fragments. I listen to the foghorns, look around the creek and the empty lot that ends in a rocky gully next to the bridge. Then I decide to walk down to Captain Cobb's for supper.

TWELVE

Cobb's is crowded, people jabbering, silverware clinking, and at first there's no place to sit. Before I can turn around and leave, a guy named Rankin—who's worked on my pickup at a gas station in Rockland—catches my eye and nods me over. He waits until I'm in range, then slides off the barstool, holding his hand out like he's ushering me.

"Thanks, man," I say.

"No problem." He winks and heads for the door. I sit down and put my cigarettes on the bar, settle in. Then this guy in a pinstriped business suit comes over.

"Excuse me, there," he says.

I look at him. He's about five-eight with a big, executive head, all trimmed and coifed. "I've been waiting my turn," he says. "My friends are all here and I've been waiting patiently for someone to leave." He gives me his best smile. "I was going to have everyone move down a seat," he says.

"Sorry about that," I say.

He waits for me to say something else. I tap a cigarette free and light up, then pick up the menu. He laughs through his nose like he can't believe what's happened and struts over to a couple other lawyer types a few seats down. They lean out from the bar to look at me. Every one of them—two men and a woman, all in business suits—is frowning. Molly comes over and I ask for a beer and a cheeseburger. She pours the beer and heads for the kitchen, stopping to turn up the tape player because it's Delbert McClinton. I tap my fingers on the bar and work on the pint until my food comes. When the burger shows up it's almost raw in the middle. But I know they're breaking in a new kid as cook. I call Molly over and part the bun and say, "Tell him to lean on it a little more next time." When she offers to send it back, I wave her off. I have another beer while I eat the undercooked burger and a pile of fries Molly provided to make up for it. I love the sweet, salty taste of fries dipped into a blob of ketchup. I take my time, keeping an eye on the lawyers. The place is still full, the pinstriped guy still doesn't have a seat. I finally push my plate away, and when Molly comes over I look in the mirror at the lawyers. "I guess I'll take one more," I tell her.

The lawyers shake their heads. One of them calls for the tab. After Molly makes change the pinstriped one says, "You know, you really ought to have some kind of a system in here."

"Excuse me?" Molly says.

"For when people are waiting for a seat." He selects a dollar from their change and drops it on the bar, then puts the rest in his pocket.

Molly looks at the dollar bill. "We do have a system."

"And what might that be?" the lawyer says.

"Generally it's first come, first served."

"Well, I was here before that fellow." He jerks his head in my direction.

"You could sue," I pipe up.

He looks at me. "I don't recall asking for your opinion."

"Or you could move a little faster," I say. "I realize that's hard to do if you're all dignified and shit."

The pinstriped guy stands up straight. "What's your name, anyway?" he says. "Do you live around here?" Then he steps back from the bar like he might be getting ready to throw down. It's kind of funny. I figure he probably takes tae-kwon-do lessons at the Y and thinks he's tough.

It gets quiet, people waiting to see what will happen.

"Come on now, Park," one of his friends says.

"I want his name," old Park insists.

"I don't blame you," I say. "*Park.*"

His face turns red and his friend says, "Let's just go."

"Don't forget your dollar," Molly says.

The lawyers look at her. Then they take their buddy Park by the arms and move him to the door. He cranes his head to stare at me, but doesn't try very hard to fight loose. After they leave the noise picks back up.

I turn back to Molly and say, " Nice crowd."

"The inn must be full," she shrugs and walks away in her cut-offs and *Captain Cobb's* t-shirt. I finish my beer and look at the clock, then I throw one of Polky's twenties down and weave my way between the tables to the door. Outside I take a look at the Lord Pequot Inn and wonder if old Park went up there. I'm tempted to follow him. But I've already decided to go out to Owls Head to see Bobby Lawson.

I walk home, jump in the pickup, and hustle back to the five-way, heading out of town. I take the bypass around Rockland to Owls Head. It's still thick fog and slow going. In Owls Head I turn onto a dirt road and lurch from rut to rut until the road peters out at a dead end. I get out and pause to piss into the underbrush.

I light a cigarette, then I head along the path through the alders. It comes out onto a ledge beside a wooded cove, where the tide is just starting to come in over the mudflats. I see cabin lights to my left, dim in the fog, Bobby's place. When I get close I see there are shingles missing and a windowpane has been replaced by plywood. I step up onto the porch and knock, and when nobody comes to the door I thump harder. I wait another few seconds, then kick the door twice, and finally it opens. A chubby, dark-haired woman looks out at me. In the hallway behind her, coats are hanging on nails and muddy boots sit on the floor. A door on the left opens and a couple kids stick their heads out and look at me. I look back at Susan and remember her with Bobby, how they used to march around high school together. I remember Bobby as a little kid, too, coming up to play with us in the canal. Sometimes he brought his brothers and sisters, but I don't remember Susan from back then.

"I need to speak to Bobby," I tell her.

"Bobb-ay ain't here."

"I saw him at the window."

"He ain't *here*."

"Listen, Susan, I'm not leaving till I talk to him."

"I'll call the cops."

"Suit yourself," I say. "I'm sure Bobby wants the cops nosing around."

The little boy and girl have come into the hallway, and now the little boy says, "Daddy's out back!"

"You be quiet, Robert!" his mother says.

I jump off the porch and trot around the cabin, past a run-down lobster boat up on blocks, and I see Bobby Lawson standing next to an old garage. The garage door has fallen loose, and inside, in the light from the back windows of the house, I can see Bobby's banged-up stock car, a maroon-and-white Chevy with the number 16 on its hood. I remember him driving a different junker while he was still in high school, becoming famous with the greaser crowd after he took third place up in Unity and got his picture in the paper. I don't know when he drove last; from the looks of #16 it's been a while.

When Bobby sees me he flinches, but then realizes I've got the jump on him and pretends to relax. "Hey there, Troy," he says as I walk up. "What brings you out to this neck of the woods?" He holds out his cigarettes. "Have a smoke."

I knock the pack out of his hand, grab him by the t-shirt, swing him in a circle, and slam him against the garage. Bobby yelps and goes limp and I let him drop to the grass, where he sucks wind on his hands and knees.

"Jesus Christ, Troy," he says when he's caught his breath. "God damn it, what the hell was that for?"

I cock a fist. "Stand up."

He holds a hand out. "You took me by surprise. I ain't in no condition to fight you now. What the hell you want to fight for, anyway?"

"You know what for."

"I got no clue, Troy!"

"Why are you hiding out back, then?"

"'Cause I know you don't like me!" His hand crabs out and finds the cigarette pack in the grass. He puts the pack in his pocket and sits back on his heels. When I lower my fist, he stands up, wheezing to show he's still in no shape to fight. "But I thought we was even," he says. "What the hell did I do now?"

"Besides rat me out to Don Moody?" I say.

Bobby sags against the shed and lights up. "Bullshit," he says. Smoke follows his words. "I don't talk to Moody about nothing." He snaps the lighter shut.

"You saw me heading out and called him up."

"Like hell," he says.

I bluff toward him and he holds his hands up and slides down to the grass again. "Look," he says, "Maybe we tangled a few years back. But I didn't tell Moody nothing."

"You better not be lying," I say.

"I wouldn't rat anybody out, Troy!"

I believe the little bastard, which pisses me off. I don't know what to do now. Finally I say, "Christ," and start off. At the corner of the house I stop and look back. He's still sitting on the ground. Behind him there's a tire hanging on a rope from an oak. "Why the hell don't you buy your kids some decent clothes?" I say.

"I do the best I can."

"Get a job," I tell him.

"I got a job."

"Digging clams?"

He crosses his arms, sits there.

I walk around the cabin to the ledge and take the path back to my truck. I drive down the dirt road to the tar road and follow it back to Pequot, but I'm not ready to go home. Instead I shoot through the square to the Lord Pequot Inn. Maybe my lawyer pals will still be there. My new friend *Park*. I swing into the parking lot at the foot of the house and look at the spot-lit old Colonial, and then I get out and walk up the stairway to the front door.

THIRTEEN

The stairway leads through a rock garden of tulips, daffodils, and bunches of little blue flowers I don't know. The flowers are all closed up. I walk up past the inn's window tables, and people looking out at me seem closed up, too. I figure with the fog they can't see the lights in the harbor and feel special. I go inside, past the desk clerk. She's the owner's daughter, and knows me, but as usual doesn't say anything. I never talk to her, either. I head on into the dining room, where an older waitress is pouring coffee. In another few weeks she'll be back in the kitchen and there'll be private-school girls waiting tables here. I like them all right as waitresses. They'll give you a peek while they set your food down, but you have to tip well or it will be the last peek you ever get.

I walk through the dining room back into the Thirsty Whale Tavern, the oldest part of the house. They've plastered the ceiling, leaving brown beams every few feet. The walls are knotty pine and there's a Maine flag in a brass holder sticking out at an angle beside the back door. It's not that big a place: there are only four bar stools, four tables, and a couch in front of the fireplace. There's a fire crackling and popping, and wood stacked in an iron holder. One of the tables is occupied by a small group that seems to be having a good time. I can tell they're flatlanders, though, without even looking at them, just from the way they're laughing. Otherwise it's not all that busy.

The bartender is wiping down the mahogany bar top. Behind him a big wood carving of a whale, painted black, hangs on the wall. Somebody's lashed a GI Joe action figure onto its back and put an olive spear in its hand.

I swing up onto a stool.

When the bartender grins, his thick mustache pulls up and you can see his gums. He's bald as an eggshell, too. "*Mister* Hull," he says. "Long time no see."

"Albert," I say, "how's the wife?"

"Still putting up with me."

"She's a saint."

"You got that right."

I lower my voice. "Any chance of a shot and a beer?"

Albert squints around the room. Then he grabs the Jack Daniels and a shot glass. He pours, sets it in front of me, twists the cap off a Budweiser. I down the whiskey and chase it with a swallow of beer while he palms the shot glass away. We have to be sneaky because the owners don't allow shooters any more, mainly because of Polky. Six months before, he'd had too many shots of Cuervo Gold after eating a big plate of shrimp and pasta, and when the whole thing came to a boil, he didn't quite make it to the bathroom. He spewed through his fingers all over a family from Nebraska. I asked him afterward why he didn't at least turn his head away, and he said it caught him by surprise. Anyway, the tourists threw up, too, after Polky's vomit puddled in their plates, and then some diners nearby joined in and pretty soon there was retching all over the place. Officially, that was the end of that, as far as drinking shooters. But Albert will still slip you one, if he trusts you, and if you're willing to listen to one of his jokes in return.

He winks at me now.

"Oh-oh," I say.

"Come on, Troy, this is a good one. This moose walks into a bar."

I roll my eyes.

"Come on," Albert says.

"Okay. Moose walks into a bar."

"Bartender looks at him and says: 'So, why the long face?'"

I raise my eyebrows and wait.

"That's it!" He says. "It's a visual!"

"Shit," I say.

Albert cackles and walks out toward the kitchen. I sip my beer and look at the GI Joe on the whale and go back to thinking about Bobby Lawson. I've known the little dink long enough to tell if he was lying, I think. So who does that leave? I can't seem to figure it. And then I feel a hand on my shoulder and I swing around.

"Captain Hull," Danny Brinker says.

I look down at him. "I didn't know you were here."

He nods toward his table. "The big shot and some of his crew. The Zeagull. Another guy from the bank. Come on over and join us."

"Thanks just the same," I say.

"Them two from the sailboat, too," he says.

I look over. Keith Zeiglaar and an older man with slicked-back hair are on one side of the table. The hot shots from the sailboat are on the other. Donald Hartley's at the head of the table. It takes a second or two to recognize him. He's laughing, showing his horsy teeth. There's another guy opposite Hartley, back to us.

"He wants to meet you," Danny says.

"Why?"

"He's been wanting to talk to a real *lobster-man*." Danny smirks when he says this, because only tourists say *lobster-man*. Whenever I hear it I imagine some dumb super-hero, walking around with a big red claw and a mask and cape. I look at the woman off the boat. She's tall and rangy, one of those blondes with dark eyebrows. Her face is tanned and when she smiles her teeth are white-white.

Danny says, "She's pretty likeable, actually."

"What about him?"

"Kind of a dickweed."

I look over at them again.

"I'll change sides," Danny says. "You can squeeze right in beside her."

"What the hell," I say. I grab my beer and follow Danny as he waddles past the big, open fireplace.

Keith Zeiglaar looks up as we come to the table.

"Mission accomplished!" Danny says.

Hartley stands up and sticks out his hand. He's a tall, well-fed guy. "Donald Hartley!" he says. "A pleasure, sir!" He's all duded up in a new flannel shirt and cargo pants from L.L. Bean. "Sit down!" he says. "You know Mr. Zeiglaar and Mr. White?"

"I know Keith," I say.

Keith says, "Trace White, Troy Hull."

Trace White is sitting up straight like a general. His slicked-back hair has gray in it. He nods an inch or two and holds his hand out. "Haven't I seen you at town meeting?" he says.

"I stopped going," I say.

He grips my hand once and lets go.

"Let me introduce you to the other folks," Hartley says. He points to the man opposite him, who has one of those mustache-and-chin beards and hair clipped so short it's like a shadow. His name is Taylor Miles. He's even more tanned than the sailor woman, and his teeth are as white as the bleached fish bones washed up on little island beaches. His grip is all fingers, and I let go quick. But then I think he's probably all right when he smiles and shrugs at me.

"And Mr. Charles Reese, my associate producer," Hartley says.

The man from the sailboat nods.

"And his lovely wife, Mallory!"

The blonde woman says, "Actually, we've met."

"Really?" Hartley says.

"Our welcome committee, remember, darling? With Danny on the boardwalk?"

"Vaguely," her husband says.

"But anyway," Mallory says, "hello again."

"Hi," I say.

"Please, sit." Hartley says.

Danny's already sitting down across from Mallory Reese. When I squeeze in beside her our legs touch and mine flinches away, which pisses me off, especially when it seems to make her smile. Then she shifts in her chair and our legs touch again, and this time I don't move. But I don't look at her, either. I look across the table at Keith Zeiglaar and Trace White. Trace White looks back at me like I'm some kind of bug.

"And how's the lobstering these days?" Hartley says. He talks kind of wet. I never noticed it on TV.

"Right poor," I tell him.

"Really? Why is that?"

"No lobsters," I say.

Danny Brinker laughs. He's taking pink shrimp from a dish in front of him, dipping them in cocktail sauce, and sucking them out of their shells.

"And do you expect things to improve?" Hartley asks.

"I keep hoping."

Hartley asks question after question, drawing me out, and before I know it I'm blabbing about how much the town has changed, how the industry is going to hell, all that stuff. I didn't intend to spout off, but I've had a fair amount to drink over the course of the day and my tongue is a little loose. And Hartley's good at his job. Even the way he drops in a cuss word every now and then, like he's talking down to my level, doesn't make me stop. I don't shut up until Mallory Reese yawns with her hand over her mouth, and all at once I realize what a blowhard I've been.

"*Excuse me!*" Mallory Reese says.

I say, "I'm sorry."

"No, no!" Hartley says. "It's good to hear it straight from the horse's mouth!" He winks at me and lowers his voice. "Cuts through the bullshit, you know?"

I scrape my chair back. "Excuse me," I say. I bolt to the bar and Albert does his sleight-of-hand thing with the Jack. I down it and tell myself not to care what a bunch of flatlanders think. I check the table and see Mallory Reese listening to Danny with her chin on her hands. I get a couple of beers from Albert and take them back. At the table Trace White has his mouth up close to Keith's ear. Keith is nodding.

I put the beer in front of Danny.

"Bless you!" Danny says.

Hartley and Reese are whispering now. Hartley pulls his head away from Reese's and shoots me this big smile. "I don't suppose you've ever been on television?" he says.

"Not that I know of," I say.

Danny laughs.

"Well," Hartley says, "I have a proposition for you. What would you say to being my guest?"

"You mean on your show?"

"Exactly."

"What for?" I say.

"We call it local color, for lack of a better term," he says. "We try and do it every stop if we can find someone. They have to be able to talk a little. And frankly, it's not a bad thing if the camera happens to like them!" He winks at me and shows his teeth.

Danny Brinker snorts beer out his nose. He picks up his napkin and blows his nose like a trumpet. "God damn it," he says. I realize then that Danny's as bad off as I am. Maybe worse. He has that bright-eyed look and his mouth has gone funny when he talks. He's not used to drinking wine. It's not the same as swilling a few beers.

"Are you all right?" Mallory Reese says.

Danny blows his nose again.

"So what do you think?" Hartley says to me. "Monday morning, five minutes or so. Just time for a few questions, and for my viewers to get to know a real Maine lobster-man."

"I have to work."

"Not a problem!" Hartley says. "We'll put in a reimbursement request." He looks at Taylor Miles.

"It might take a week," Miles says, "knowing them."

"But it'll happen," Hartley says. "So what do you say?"

"Thanks just the same," I say.

Hartley wags a finger at me. "I'm afraid that's not acceptable. One thing you should know is I simply won't take no for an answer." He grins, but his finger is still wagging. "Trust me on this," he says.

Taylor Miles says, "He really won't."

"Now, we don't need to rehearse more than a minute or two," Hartley says. "It'll be painless, I promise. We're broadcasting from the town dock. If you can come in at six-thirty we can discuss what I might say to introduce you."

I look at Danny. He shrugs.

Hartley winks and says, "Good." Then he puts his hand on Reese's shoulder. "Charles," he says. "I need your advice."

"Surely," Reese says.

Hartley leans close and starts whispering again. I've never seen such people for whispering. Then he stands up and says, "Let's go outside. A little perspective." Taylor Miles jumps up when Reese does, and the three of them step away from the table. When Trace White coughs into his hand, Hartley says, "Oh yes, Mr. White, come along with us. Mr. Zeiglaar, you too. By all means. Troy?"

"I'm fine," I say.

"I know better than to ask the lovely Mallory," Hartley says with a laugh.

She smiles at him.

Reese looks down his beak at her and says, "I'll be right back."

"Enjoy yourself, darling."

Hartley leads his little gang out through the dining room.

"So there you go," Danny says to me.

"There I go where?"

"Straight to Hollywood. I can see it now."

Mallory smiles.

"Don't forget all us little people," Danny says.

"Maybe we should get his autograph," Mallory says. She's squinting up at me. She seems very close. Our legs are still touching, even though there's plenty of room at the table now. I wonder what's going on.

"Too late," Danny says. "He's gonna be rich and won't speak to folks like us. He's gonna buy himself a mansion out in Hollywood."

"But he's blushing," Mallory says. "Maybe there's hope."

My face is hot, and I can't think of anything to come back with, so I just finish my beer and stand up.

"Was it something we said?" Danny grins.

"I have to get home."

"Sure you do!"

Mallory smiles at me, her eyes crinkling.

I escape back to the bar and deal out some cash for Albert. He points his finger at me like a pistol. I head for the back door by the fireplace. I can feel Mallory watching and have to be careful not to scuff my feet. Outside it's still foggy as hell. I walk down a crushed-rock driveway to the parking lot, cussing myself out. Fucking *swanks*. I climb into the pickup and slam the door, and look up at the deck that runs around the left side of the old house. Hartley, Reese, White, and Taylor Miles are up there smoking cigars. Hartley has a cigar in one hand and the other arm out, like he's casting a spell over the town. Everyone else is listening. Then Keith Zeiglaar comes onto the deck from inside. He has a cigar going, too.

I back out of the parking spot and goose it, squawking the tires. I head down the street and across the river to the square. I'm still thinking about Mallory Reese. I can still feel her leg against mine, and as I cross the square to Seaview Street I almost miss the county cruiser, coming out of a side street farther up Main, turning toward me like a shark in the water.

FOURTEEN

For drinking and driving you need good cop-sense. I've spotted them two streets over between buildings, seen them reflected in traffic mirrors, dodged them one way or another all over Midcoast Maine. But tonight I almost blow it. The cruiser just doesn't register at first. I'm turning across the square and see him coming out of Elm Street a couple of blocks up, but it takes a second before I think: Christ, that's a cop! Maybe the fog is partly responsible. Anyway, I do the exact wrong thing by speeding up to get out of sight. My muffler has a little rust hole and when I accelerate it gets loud. I don't remember that until I'm scooting across the square and the muffler does its noisy fluttery thing, and I have to figure the sheriff will hear it and come after me. So I punch the truck around the post office and onto the little side street that runs uphill, and I pull into an alley that's hard to see because of a crabapple in the backyard of the restaurant that fronts on Seaview. I roll down the window and hear the cruiser speed past below, heading up Seaview Street.

I give him a minute and then reverse and coast back down to Seaview, where I cut the engine and listen. Across the street, the brick block with the restaurant and shops is dark. Fog hangs on everything. I can't hear the cruiser, and I figure he's had time to get up to Hull Street and start back, so he probably thinks I headed down the peninsula. I turn the key and bump over the edge of the curb onto Seaview.

Easy, boy, I think.

I drive along the flat part of Seaview Street, past the tourist shops, then uphill past the yacht club. There's a security spotlight on there, and the stepladder still leans against the wall. I keep on going. It's nerve-wracking, heading through the soup toward where the cruiser disappeared. I could park somewhere and walk up and not have to worry about it, but that seems like too much trouble.

At the top of the hill I don't see him. I drive down Hull and he's not there, either, so I let out my breath and pull into the yard, and nearly wipe out Polky's Harley sitting on its kickstand at the edge of the driveway.

Polky's sitting on a folding chair with his big boots up on the bench that runs around the deck. He's smoking one of those little wine-flavored cigars. I can smell it. There's a whiff of pot in the air, too, and I figure he burned one before I showed up. Out on the creek the fog sits smack-dab on the water. He turns and looks at me as I climb up the steps.

"Hey, brother," he says.

"Make yourself at home," I say.

"Don't worry, I did." He holds up his can of PBR. "Hey, you almost had some more company, too." He wags the beer an inch toward the driveway.

"Knox County's finest?"

"How'd you know?"

"I happened to be *evading* him."

"No shit?" Polky laughs. "He came by wicked slow, all the way to the dead end. Then he went back the same way. Stopped by the driveway. Then down and across the bridge and out the peninsula." He looks at me. "You don't seem *too* bad off."

"It doesn't take much."

"Not these days," Polky says.

I open the door to go inside and Polky says, "Thanks, I'd love another."

I grab a couple of cans out of the fridge and take them onto the deck. I hand one to Polky and move the other folding chair close and sit down like him, with my feet on the bench. I look out into the yard.

He takes a big hit of the beer, and I say, "Give me one of those cigars."

Polky takes the box out of his vest and a pack of matches and tosses them onto the table. He hooks his hands behind his head and watches me peel one out of its wrapper. "So'd you make your payment all right?" he says.

"Thanks to you."

Polky waves it off. "How about the next one?"

"I'm working on it," I say. The matchbook is damp, so I wipe it on my t-shirt, but still some of the match head comes off. I have to turn the match and pop it quick under my finger to make it flare. I draw the flame into the cigar and when it's going, toss the match off the deck. Then I suck in a lungful of cigar smoke—I inhale everything, even if it hurts.

"Listen, they're gonna take it away from you," Polky says.

"Don't be so dramatic," I say.

"You know they are."

I blow smoke out.

"There ain't much on the water anymore," he says. "There's Charlie's and yours. Everything else has already been snapped up." He leans forward and points at me. "See, this place is too good for an asshole like you. Some *lawyer* should be living here, some fucking swank, not a dumb-ass lobster fisherman like you. Right now they're figuring out the best way to get you the hell out, Troy. Then they'll plow this house under and build something modern. They'll put up their No Trespassing signs along the road. They'll post the other side, too, so nobody can have picnics on the rocks and kids won't make a lot of noise. They'll put in a tennis court, private use only. If you come up the creek with a dip net, they'll walk down and stare at you to let you know you ain't welcome." He sits back with a little grunt. "Tell me where I'm wrong."

I can't. Every day I see more glassy new mansions along the shore. And they're always posted. You have to go twenty or thirty miles inland to hunt any more.

"I really don't give a rat's ass about you," Polky says, "but I'd hate to have to give up admiring the flowers or taking a swim or watching the damn birds or whatnot."

I laugh and puff on the cigar. The peepers are sounding from the boggy spot between the house and the dock. I take one last hit and pitch the cigar out onto the lawn. Polky does the same with his. Then he says, "You're letting them set you up."

"I get the message, okay?"

"Shut up and listen. You're in trouble, but I can help you out." He pops his knuckles in order, from first finger to pinkie, then does it on the other hand, while he thinks about what to say. "You might not know it," he says, "being the stupid shit that you are. You probably think there's some way out, and all you got to do is come up with it. But listen, Troy, since you're already in default and they've served you notice, all they got to do is tell you to pay it all off. Probably the only reason they haven't is it's too soon after they took Charlie's house and they don't want to look bad. But they're going to, Troy-boy."

"Say you're right. There's nothing I can do about it."

"Bullshit. How much you got left to pay?"

"Too much."

"How *much?*"

"Ninety-five or so."

Polky nods, and his long hair shakes. "All right," he says, "that ain't so bad. That sounds like a lot, but it ain't actually all that much money. You and me can pay that off pretty quick."

"Listen, Bill . . . " I start to say.

"No, you listen. They got everybody else out except you, and now they're fixing to get you out, too." He stands up and puts his hands on the railing. "It *is* pretty nice out here," he says. "You'd think a man would do what he had to do."

"Everybody's not like you," I say.

He spits off the deck.

I stand up beside him. The fog sits on the water and in the trees. I can't see across to the other side. It's funny how much the fog seems to *weigh*. We stand there together while a car *whumps* onto the bridge, crosses the bridge, and *whumps* off, following Seaview back into town. Its tires sound sticky on the wet pavement.

"There he goes," Polky says.

"Yep."

He turns all of a sudden and punches me in the shoulder, hard enough to tip me onto one leg. "Asshole!" he says. "I'll be in touch." Then he stomps across the deck, down the steps, and over to his bike. He kick-starts the Harley, backs it around with baby steps, toes it into gear, and rips out of the driveway and along to the corner. I hear him gear down, sputtering and coughing, then head down over the hill.

I go inside, grab another beer, and take it outside. There's a lot churning around in me. I'm gloomy and excited at the same time. It's starting to feel like I will join up with Polky sooner or later. Maybe the warp run changed me, who the hell knows? Maybe I'm different now that I've *done* it, even if I didn't know I was doing it.

I finish my beer and open another. When a car comes up Seaview and turns down Hull, I figure it might be the sheriff again, so I move my chair out of sight from the street. But the car comes right into my driveway. I go inside and shut the door and stand there in the dark, trying to decide what to do if he knocks on the door.

The car door *chunks* shut, and light, quick steps come toward the house on the crushed rock. It sounds like a female, and for a second I wonder if it's Dickless Tracy come by to settle the score for calling her a split-tail. But it doesn't sound like some tough woman. It sounds softer. I listen to her come up the steps and my heart starts hammering. For no good reason I think it might just be Julie Marie, coming home.

FIFTEEN

But it's not Julie Marie, it's Niki Harjula skipping up the steps. I try not to feel too disappointed. She has her head down and her hands in her pockets and is halfway across the deck when I pull the slider open. It makes her jump, and she puts a hand to her breast.

"Oh!" she says.

"Sorry," I say. "Have a seat, I'll grab you a beer." In the kitchen I look at my mother's sunflower clock. I'm surprised that it's after midnight already.

"I like your deck," Niki says when I come back out. "Last time I was here you still had the porch."

I hand her the beer. "It's been that long?"

"Years," she says, and laughs.

We sit down at the table. "So what's up?"

"I just didn't feel like going home." She takes a small sip of beer and puts the can down.

"I was out tonight, too," I say, and when she looks up I tell her about leaving the inn and the hole in my muffler and dodging the cruiser. I try to get her to laugh, but she just keeps looking at me.

"What?" I say.

"You don't need an OUI right now," she says.

"Tell me about it."

"I mean you *really* don't."

"What's going on?"

"Can we walk down to the crick?"

I smile at her pronunciation—a leftover from her trailer park days, and it's kind of charming because she doesn't notice that she does it.

"Will you be warm enough?"

"Sure."

We walk down past the willow and the elms and the little bog and along to the dock. We sit on the end of the dock with our feet hanging, just like old times. There's no traffic now and no birds. It's quiet enough to hear the water dancing by. It's still foggy as hell—you can feel it on your face.

I lift my beer a little too fast and hit myself in the teeth. These last couple might have done the trick and I take a more careful sip.

"Troy?" she says.

"Niki?" I try to be funny.

"Cut it out."

"Sorry," I snicker, but she doesn't laugh. She sticks her hands between her thighs and says, "Troy, listen, I think something fishy is going on at the bank."

"What kind of something?" I say.

"Keith had a little meeting this afternoon. Trace White, Donald Hartley, and Danny Brinker. They all ran down to Keith's office and then Keith buzzed me to say he wasn't taking any calls."

"That's quite a collection."

"Isn't it?"

"So what was the occasion?"

"I don't really know. I listened at the door, but I couldn't stand there very long. I'm pretty sure I heard your name, though."

"They were talking about me?"

"Unless you know another Troy Hull."

I try to think, which isn't very easy at the moment. "Well," I say, "I ran into that same crowd at the inn tonight. They were yapping about putting a *lobster-man* on the show. *Me*, believe it or not. Maybe you heard them talking about that."

"Maybe," Niki says, "but there's the other thing, too."

"What other thing?"

"Did you hear who bought Charlie's house?"

"Nope."

"It was Hartley." She waits, and after a moment I get where she's going. I've seen the swanks do it before: buy up two or three properties to make one of their own. Then they call them *compounds.*

"Kind of a small lot," I say. Niki raises her eyebrows. I turn the whole deal over in my mind, let it mix with the beer fumes. Then I think of something else. "You said Danny was part of this little get-together?"

"Yep," Niki says.

"He seems to be popping up a lot."

"How so?"

"Well, he was at the pound before we went to Scotia," I say, and when she says, "Scotia?" I take a minute to fill her in on the warp run, without mentioning Polky's little side deal. I hear the foghorns hooting out in the harbor. For some reason I haven't noticed them for a while, though they must have been blowing the whole time.

"You went *smuggling?* With *Polky?*" Niki says.

"Just rope," I say.

"Wicked bad idea," she says.

"I needed the cash."

"Now you *sound* like Polky."

"I don't care."

"But you're better than him."

"Yeah?" I say. "And what does that get me?"

"It isn't supposed to get you anything," Niki says. She sounds disappointed, and I remember she got pretty uptight after turning her life around. I mean, she pulled a one-eighty, pretty much. I used to think it was funny.

"Whatever," I say. "Anyway, my point is the clam cops were waiting for us when we got back, like somebody tipped them off. And Danny was there. And then Danny's at the inn tonight, and I almost get busted when I leave." I look at Niki. This close, I can see the tiny fuzz on her cheek, and suddenly I want to lean over and kiss it. That's when I know I'm drunk. I look at her face, and then I remember I'm trying to work something out and finally I say, "I'm probably full of shit. I can't think good enough to figure anything out tonight."

"Okay," Niki says. "I'll keep my eyes open."

"Deal."

"But no more *smuggling*."

"Yes, boss."

We sit listening to the water. Then Niki squirms and says, "My butt's asleep," and we stand up. She crosses her arms and we look out at the fog.

"Remember the canal?" she says.

"Yeah, I was over there today."

"How was it?"

"Wet."

Niki laughs. "Remember those baby birds?"

We were six or seven and we found three baby shags dead in their stick-and-mud nest on the rocks by the canal. We picked them up, and their necks dangled from our hands. Then we put them back and ran to tell my folks. I remember the old man explaining that if *all* the little shags grew up there wouldn't be any fish, and my mother saying, "Ernest, for God's sake," and telling us that sometimes little shags played dead to fool people who might want to take them home. And I remember how after lunch we ran back and the baby shags were gone.

Niki smiles at me, sticks her fingers in her pockets, and sort of wanders off the dock toward the house. I follow her and stumble over the roots that break the surface along the path. Niki laughs and we walk on up to the driveway and lean against her car. I sling an arm around her and she wrinkles up her nose, smiling like a cute little kid.

I notice the foghorns again, and I'm trying to figure which is which when Niki turns and reaches up to put her arms around my neck. She pulls my head down and kisses me. It's so sudden it takes me a moment to notice it's different from kissing Julie Marie: Niki's shorter and stronger in my arms, and she keeps her tongue in her own mouth. I think I like it that way. My hand seems to move all by itself up her ribs, and when I touch her breast her breathing gets noisy and she leans away with her eyes wide open, staring up at me.

"Don't look at me," I say. "I didn't start it."

She ducks her head against my chest and laughs. Then she raises her face again. Our hands roam around and we squirm against each other and I realize that if this keeps up we might just head inside and jump into the bed I haven't used since Julie Marie left.

And that's when I start to chicken out.

I think about Julie Marie and that bed, and the way it was at the end, and before I know it I'm worrying that it might be the same with Niki, and I start to lose my steam. She picks up on it and leans back again to look at me. I shift my weight and hold onto her elbows and I try to think of what to say. But how the hell do you explain something like this to a girl?

"Niki," I finally say. But then I'm stuck again.

She waits just so long, and when I still can't think of how to proceed, she steps back and smoothes the front of her jacket with her hands. Then she clears her throat and says, "All right, good to go."

"Niki," I say again. But that's as far as I get.

"I'm okay," she says. "It's all right."

"No," I say, but she holds up a hand.

"You don't owe me anything, Troy Hull," she says. She's keeping her voice light, but her eyes are blinking like mad.

"What?" I say.

"You don't *owe* me anything."

That's so far from what I'm thinking that it makes me even more tongue-tied. "I know," I say, but that finishes it. All the cogs in my brain are slipping and clanking, and she's not about to stick around waiting.

"Morning comes early!" She smiles like I'm a customer at the bank, then opens the car door, sits down, and hikes her legs in. She pulls the door shut, rolls down the window, and looks up at me. She smiles, but her eyes are wet. "Oh, jeez," she says. Then she rolls the window up. She backs out and drives away through the fog.

SIXTEEN

I wake up to church bells, and at first I think I'm fooling myself, like with the bulldozer. But then I remember I never set my alarm because you can't haul on Sundays anyway. I listen to the bells and think about last night. I think about waking up with Niki this morning, with the bells ringing. It's hard to picture—after all, I've never slept with anyone but Julie Marie. Mr. Experience, that's me. Maybe if things had worked out with Niki, though. Maybe it'd be like the bells were ringing for us. I remember how she felt in my arms: sturdy and strong. But I decide it's just as well that we didn't go through with it. What if we tried and I *did* peter out again? I don't want Niki thinking I'm some kind of an invalid.

I need to think about something else, and I put my hands behind my head and think about Danny Brinker. I don't get any farther than I did last night and then I conjure up Charlie Hamalainen. I remember something about Charlie, how he got busted for OUI coming home from playing bingo at the Legion Hall. He used to go there to meet women of a certain age. He'd sit in his truck and drink a six-pack and then go in and charm the ladies. But one night they were waiting for him when he left. They caught him dead to rights and it didn't help him any when they decided to come after his house a little later on.

And what about Hartley asking me to be on his TV show? I can't figure that any more than I can figure it about Niki. I give up and roll over and lift the shade and look out at more goddamn fog.

I finally crawl out of bed an hour later. Downstairs in the kitchen I start a pan of water heating. When it's boiling, I breathe in the steam, letting it clear my head. Then I poach a couple of eggs and make toast. I eat on the deck, watching the birds. After breakfast I put my dishes in the sink and leave the house and walk down to the corner. Near the corner I stop for a peek at Charlie's lot. It's a sad-looking scene with the house gone. I look at it for a while and head down the hill toward town. The fog is shifting around and I can see the sun through it. I hear people talking and look between two houses at the Congo Church, where the service has ended and everybody's coming outside. I stop long enough to check out the little girls and boys in their Sunday clothes, and then continue on to the five-way, and cut across to the drugstore—*MAINE-LY DRUGS*, it says on the window. It's an old place that still has a soda fountain. I grab a *Sunday Telegram*, pay the chubby kid at the register, and head back up the hill. At the house I take a big mug of coffee and the paper out to the deck and spend the morning in the wicker rocker. The fog breaks up and the sun comes out for real as I read through the paper. I read everything, even *Parade*, and catch up on the news. I read that one of the Kennedy nephews is in trouble for trying to screw some waitress who didn't want to be screwed. I feel sorry for the waitress, but I wish I had that kind of confidence. Next time, maybe I ought to just take the plunge and see what happens. Maybe I should ride up to Augusta, go bar-hopping, and see if someone wants to take me home.

I have a couple tuna sandwiches for lunch and walk out through the field to the woods. I hike into the woods and along the old mule-path beside the canal. The leaves are still new on the hardwoods, and more light comes through than in summer.

I break away from the trail, cross to the old Hull graveyard. It's getting overgrown, and I'll have to come up with the mower. I wander around, looking at the headstones, mostly slate tablets. A lot of the lettering has worn off, but I can read some dates from the 1700s and a few Finnish names. No one's been buried here for a long time. It's illegal to have family cemeteries now, and I had to bury my parents across town. I probably should go over there and visit them more often, but I feel them stronger here.

I tell my troubles to the folks, trying not to sound too whiny, and then walk over to our dog Sam's little marker and think about him for a while. Then I go back to the mule path and home. I spend the afternoon watching the NBA playoffs and drinking more coffee. All the while my thoughts go round and round about my folks and Julie Marie and Niki and everything that's happened to me.

Eventually I'm coffeed out and I go out onto the deck with a frostie. I've put it off because drinking on top of a hangover is bad business. But it's goddamn tasty and my spirits lift a bit. I look out at the creek: shags all over the place, seagulls, a big brown-and-white fishhawk diving into the water, then lifting up with a fish, shaking the water off his feathers.

The birds put on a show until some little kids arrive, throwing rocks and sticks into the water from the opposite bank of the creek. There's a path that comes up from the far side of the bridge, one of our old secret trails. The kids have a girl with them, an older sister or maybe a nanny—the swanks in Pequot love their nannies. This one is keeping a close eye on the kids.

An hour later more company arrives, two men in a green canoe wearing puffy orange lifejackets. They wave to the kids and the nanny and go all the way up to where the creek comes out of the woods. Then they turn around and let the current bring them back. They wave to the kids again and drift down under the bridge. Then the nanny opens her backpack and spreads out a snack on the ledge. I like watching the little kids and the no-nonsense girl keeping them in line. After they eat, they pack up their stuff and leave. Then the birds come back. The shags skid into their landings on the water, the fish hawks big-flap to their little perches. Later, when the fog comes back and it gets damp, I go inside and balance my checkbook. It's only off by fifty-odd dollars—not bad after six months—and it's in my favor.

"What do you know about that?" I say out loud.

I put the checkbook in the junk drawer, wash all the dishes in the sink, and run the vacuum over the floors. I do a couple loads of laundry. When it gets dark I have a couple more sandwiches and another beer. I try the tube, but there's nothing on, so I pull out a family picture album. They're old pictures passed down to my parents. There's a shot of my grandfather Hull, his wife, and thirteen kids posing in front of the creek, dressed for church, looking proud and itchy at the same time. It makes me wish I lived back then, when nobody thought it was all right to take your house away. It makes me wish I had a few brothers and sisters, too. I look closer and notice shags in the water behind them.

I look through other albums. They took a lot of pictures of me. My mom couldn't have more kids, so they didn't have a choice. There I am, laughing on the old man's shoulders; in my high chair, my mother spooning some kind of goop into my mouth; in this or that boat; with my gang looking out from the canal, just our heads showing; playing hoops; graduating high school.

I flip through all six albums and put them away. Then I tramp upstairs and undress for bed. The sheets are cool and it's a comfort to stretch out my legs and feel the top sheet pull at my toes. I lie in the dark, tired but not sleepy yet, and try to sort through things, but I'm starting to feel overloaded. It's not enough that the lobsters aren't crawling. It's not enough that the bank is after me. And the cops.

I know I'm making too much of it. After all, I never had any problems before. Part of it is Julie Marie and part of it is never doing it with anyone else.

Simple.

After some time I make myself stop thinking about it. I don't know how long it's been, and I don't dare look at the clock because if it's too late it'll make me anxious and I'll never get to sleep. I know from past experience that if I just lie there, eventually it will happen, and it does, sometime during the wee hours.

SEVENTEEN

The next morning I'm up early and for some reason there's a bounce back in my step, even though nothing's changed: it's *still* thick of fog, and I still haven't gotten laid, and they're still after my house, and I still didn't sleep all that well. There are times when you just wake up and feel all right. I check the thermometer—forty-seven degrees—and load the coffee maker. I boil eggs, fry bacon. When it's all done I take my breakfast out onto the deck. It's a little cool, not quite daybreak. The shags are working hard, diving after *their* breakfast. There are three fish hawks in the tall trees across the creek.

I take my dishes in, fill my thermos, make sandwiches, and head out the side door, grabbing my boots along the way. I cross the driveway and head in my bare feet across the lawn to the dock. The cold, wet grass makes my toes ache a little. I drift out and start rowing, pulling swirls in the water. It's about half-tide, going out. I work the oars as quietly as I can, and the skiff speeds past Charlie Hamalainen's empty lot and under the bridge into the foggy harbor. There's nothing going on at the marina yet. I notice Polky's boat is gone.

On the *Julie Marie* I dry my feet on my sweatshirt and tug on my socks. I put on my rubber boots and bend the tops over. The whole time I'm listening to the weatherman on the radio. There's a small-craft warning, maybe a squall or thunderstorm, which is okay because it might clear the goddamn fog away. I motor out toward the harbor island, ride between the island—so wrapped in fog I can barely see the spruce—and Danny's and out into the bay. I have a thermos-cap of coffee in my hand and I try to enjoy the quiet before it's time to grab the gaff and start working.

It's the same deal with the fog: by mid-morning it has drawn back to the islands and the sun is shining. The temperature is in the low sixties and it feels good to work up a sweat. But my mood has gone a little sour because I'm still not catching anything to speak of. Somehow I thought that my luck would have to change, but no dice.

I break early for a sandwich, throw out the anchor, and cut the engine. Then I sit out in the sunshine, back against the transom. When I peel the wax paper off a sandwich, gulls that have been trailing me all morning light on the wheelhouse roof. One is a big old black back. I don't mind the black backs, and I toss him a piece of bread. This guy's been through the mill, scars around his eyes, a toe missing. He's more beat up than I am. He works the bread around with his bill and eats it, while the other gulls watch. I drink coffee and take another bite of sandwich. I shut my eyes and turn my face up. The boat rocks like a big cradle. I finish my sandwich and put the ball of waxed paper back in my lunch bucket. Then I hear Polky's boat, steaming out from Owls Head. He has the fastest boat in Mid-coast Maine and it sounds like nobody else's. I watch him come up, looking like a toy at first. When he gets close the seagulls fly over, but Polky isn't fishing so they head off toward shore—they've had it with both of us. Polky idles his engine and drifts up. He's wearing jeans and a green-and-white t-shirt, and his beard is all bushy from the damp air.

Polky.

I met him in first grade, running around like a little Indian kid, which he was, partly. Everybody wanted to be his best friend, but I forked over my *Lone Ranger* pencil box. After a while he was at Hull Creek almost as much as Niki. We played in the skiff, fished in the creek, ran around the dry canal, did our sneaky stuff. When we were older, my father let us shoot his .22 at paper-plate targets. We played Little League baseball, joined Booster's Club, played basketball. We got pretty good at basketball, and senior year won an Eastern Maine championship. I remember Polky ripping rebounds away from taller kids, never backing off an inch. I remember they put us on fire trucks and drove down Main Street to celebrate. I grin back at him across twenty feet of water.

"You again?" I say.

"It's a free ocean," he says.

"Plenty of room on it, too."

"Fuck you," he says, smiling.

I hold up my thermos.

"No thanks." He hooks his hands on the wheelhouse roof, kind of hangs there. "So I'm asking," he says. "I've got something pretty good. I could use some help."

"No thanks," I say.

"You don't sound too sure." Polky scratches his chin with his claw, hangs from just one arm. He's a handsome dude, with a big, straight nose and bright teeth. His eyes are a little sleepy unless he gets pissed and then they roll up into his head. But now he's got the lazy look. "Listen," he says. "Sooner or later you'll see the light. I can wait a little while. But things are coming together." He grins. The boat goes up and down.

"I told you no," I say.

"Yeah, but you didn't mean it." He looks over his shoulder, puts a foot up on his rail, and leans on his raised knee. "You ain't got any choice," he says.

We look at each other.

"What about you?" I say. "Ever think about going back to fishing?"

"*Just* fishing?"

"Yeah."

He drops his head and laughs. "I think about winning the lottery, too."

"But you must be ahead of the game by now."

"I got a lot of overhead."

"But you're doing okay."

"Fair to middling."

"So why don't you quit?"

Polky wrinkles up his nose. "You think I'm corrupt, Troy-boy, and I ought to get out. But what I do ain't no more crooked than what those *businessmen* in town do." He jerks his thumb toward Pequot. "Every goddamn day of the year."

"Guys like that have connections," I say.

"I'll get them too, when I've got enough money."

"If you make it that far."

"Listen, Troy, you got to ignore the consequences. That's the only way you can be as crooked as they are. They think up the rules for people like us, and if you let 'em get away with it, you're screwed." He laughs. "Besides, it keeps the old blood flowing."

"*That* I believe."

Polky salutes with his claw and grabs the wheel. He reaches down for the key, but then holds off, looking over at me. "You haven't got a sparkplug wrench on board, do you? I got to pull a couple in my truck."

"Not on board," I say.

"How about in the Bat-Truck?" He calls it that because he claims you can find anything you need in my pickup if you rummage around long enough.

"Maybe in the toolbox," I say.

"I'll take a look." He fires up the *Lainey P* and heads off, throwing a plume of water as he steers across the bay. I cap the thermos and go back to work, hauling my traps, baiting, moving on. Polky's point of view tugs at me the whole time, though: why *should* you try to be honest when nobody else does? It's too bad you have to make that choice. Too bad they wouldn't just leave you the hell alone. If you could just do your work, live where you grew up, and be left alone. I wonder what exactly Polky has in mind. It would be nice to have some cash. But what if it went bad? What if he's free-lancing again and gets in trouble? Or what if we get caught? I could lose my house and boat that way as easily as making late payments to the bank. And go to jail for a decade or so, to top it off. Besides, I think, it's probably something more serious than pot, if it's going to be that big a score. And there are enough messed up people running around without making more of them.

I lean over the rail to hook the line and yank it up over the snatch block. But Polky's voice won't go away. He's like the little devil on your shoulder. I get so distracted thinking about his arguments that I almost don't notice when the weather changing. But then the breeze picks up and I see dark clouds near the horizon and all of a sudden I remember the small-craft warning from that morning and I forget all about Polky.

"Oopsie," I say.

I push my last trap astern and spin the wheel, lighting a cigarette for the ride in, hoping I came to in time. The clouds are whipping up fast, and I keep an eye on them as I open her up and race for the pound.

EIGHTEEN

The air smells different when I pop out of Stan's office and the breeze has already come up. I hustle down to the float and work the *Julie Marie*'s lines. She parts company with the float as if she's as eager to get going as I am, and I jump aboard and feed her the gas. We bump out the harbor and sort of squirt through the turbulent water between the lighthouse point and Monroe. When I clear the point, the water has gone thick and rough, whitecaps blowing off the tops of the waves, which travel away from the boat in peaks. I look at the hills, at clouds dragging showers like veils toward the bay. I start across in front of the smoky stacks of the fish-processing plant in Rockland and for a second the sun breaks through and shines off the metal roof of the plant and the whitewashed Coast Guard station next door, where big iron buoys are drydocked, lying on their sides on the pier.

Then the clouds close back in. Pretty quick it's gloomy and gusty.

The showers start and in ten minutes the whole bay starts to bubble. I'm running parallel to the shore, taking the seas off my port side, but then the squall just *explodes*, and after one scary roll I turn straight into it, figuring I'd better wait it out in the lee of the breakwater. I struggle along that way, catching sight of the granite wall every time I crest a wave, but before long I change my mind again. The boat's just getting pounded too hard. I can't run ahead of it either, because if I hit a trough wrong I'll drive the bow too far under. Or I'll hit a ledge or something. I decide there's only one way out of this and that's to head for home again and try and keep as much of the squall on my shoulder as possible.

It's nerve-wracking, trying to work the bow into the wind. I turn the wheel and the *Julie Marie* rolls way over and I try to stay calm and fight to keep it stable. Every third or forth wave bulges up like a wall, passes under the boat, bobs me around like a cork, then drops me into a deep trough for the next one. Sheets of cold rain fling themselves into the wheelhouse. I work the throttle, trying to time the surges, and we wallow along toward Pequot. I can hear the wind whining past the antennas and it's frightening. I have to ignore my doubts and just keep going, trust it'll work out.

After a long while, though, I catch a break and the squall's energy seems to let up. I make some good progress before it comes back fierce and I have to play it careful again. Then it lets up once more and I run hard for home. The rain slacks off and clouds tatter open so I can see pieces of blue sky. I can see more coming over the hills, but I manage to punch into Pequot Harbor before it hits. A big wave carries me in like a surfer. Then I'm right in it again, tossing around. The waves are all over the place, coming from about six directions. It takes me three tries to snag the mooring and pull the skiff up to the boat. Two inches of water are washing a Styrofoam cup around inside the skiff, and I'm totally soaked, but I feel pretty good, all the same. I wipe the rain out of my eyes and make sure there's plenty of room between the *Julie Marie* and Polky's boat, then I tie off and move around the boat, looking for damage. All I see is a small ding in the transom. I grab everything that's still loose and throw it down into the cuddy. I manage to lower myself into the skiff without capsizing and dig toward the bridge in the rain, trying the whole way not to swamp. Eventually I come out from under the bridge and push along the swollen creek up to my dock. I pull the skiff onto the dock, tie it upside down, and run for the house, boots squishing. There's a snapping noise, the wind flapping my curtains through an open window, and I lunge inside, yank the curtains in, and shut the window. I kick my boots off, leaving my sopping clothes in a pile on the floor, and walk bare-assed around the house, shutting the rest of the windows. I take an onion out of the fridge, peel the loose skin, and eat it like an apple on my way upstairs. I drop the core into the toilet and turn on the shower, staying in until the chill is gone from my bones. Then I put on clean jeans and t-shirt and go back downstairs. I slice another onion and make myself a giant BLT. I take a moment to give thanks to Old Man Ollsen for building such a stout boat. Then I take the sandwich and a glass of milk into the living room. The rain is drumming hard, gusts working at the windows. But the old house is stout, too. I wonder about my traps, and then I go back to work on the sandwich, finishing it just as the thunder and lightning start. The wind howls, swaying the tall trees, and I worry I might lose one. Lightning stutters, then blinks out, and there's a crash that shakes the house. Pretty soon it's like I'm under attack. The storm rampages for fifteen minutes, booming like cannons, flashing like I don't know what. Then, as fast as it came, the storm moves on, and pretty soon I can't see any lightning at all and there are only far-off rumbles of thunder.

As soon as the sun comes out, I go outside. Everything smells fresh and clean and steam drifts up off the water. There are no trees down. I pick up my rocker and the folding chairs and brush leaves off their seats. Then I decide to check things out, and I back the pickup onto Hull Street and drive over branches and soaked leaves to the crossing. I park in Charlie's driveway, walk across Seaview to the harbor, and see the *Julie Marie* riding high and dry. The *Lainey P* has come through it all right, too. They look nice in the sunlight slanting along Danny's marina. I look downtown and see the blue sailboat blown onto its side. It's a shock, like rounding a curve and coming upon a car accident.

I'm sure what happened was the wind came whipping up the harbor and built up a series of big waves that pulled the stern down enough for them to slam in and eventually swamp her. Which is exactly what Freddie had warned Reese about. *Dumb bloody swank.* But then I tell myself to get off my high horse. I wasn't any genius myself today.

Erky Jura's launch is out by the sailboat, getting ready to tow it in, and I see Erky waiting on his dock with his baseball cap back on his head. I walk back to the pickup and head downtown for a closer look, following the rainwater rushing along the curb toward the square. At the landing I see there's a trash can over and seagulls flap away from the mess as I drive up, squawking at the interruption. I look for Eddy Cranberry—who's usually Johnny-on-the-spot when it comes to picking up the landing—but then I remember he's scared of thunder and lightning, so he's probably still hiding under his bed.

I watch Erky's boys tow the sailboat to his dock. Then I hear voices and turn to see Tommy Winchenbach leading a couple of sightseers onto the boardwalk. Tommy's a retired native who used to own a house on Seaview Street, but lost it when his taxes got too high. Now he spends his time bullshitting the tourists. He must have come out after the storm and managed to scare up a couple of clients.

They walk up, Tommy in front, then a chubby woman with a big-lensed camera, and a man bringing up the rear, swinging his arms. Winchenbach is holding forth in an overcooked Maine accent he likes to use, but he shuts up long enough for the woman to take pictures of the blue sailboat, which Erky's boys are now pulling upright with a winch. Then Tommy starts in again, telling about the famous poet who used to live in Pequot. "Oh, she'd run right through town," he says, and waves a hand. "Ayuh! All the way up the mountain."

The tourists look up at the mountain.

"Right up the side!" Winchenbach says. "There warn't any road back then, see?" He shuts his eyes, quotes a few lines about mountains, woods, and bays. Then he squints at the tourists and rubs his chin whiskers, like he might just spout some more poetry. I laugh, because I know the words are on a plaque up on the mountain by the old tower.

Winchenbach sneaks me a look.

"Imagine!" the man says, "Hearing her quoted at the public landing!"

"This is the real Americana!" the woman says.

"The Maine mystique!" the man says.

"This is better than William Least Heat Moon, darling," she says. "We should start a journal!" They smile at each other, and the man takes the woman's arm and brings her close. They turn their heads so their visors won't hit, and whisper.

Winchenbach looks sideways at me again. I wink at him.

The tourists finish up and ask if Tommy might consider joining them for dinner, so they can talk more about the famous dead poet.

Winchenbach says, "Don't see why not."

They walk off, Winchenbach giving me the finger behind his back.

I look out at the harbor. It's still breezy and the sailboats bob around like toys. Down at Erky's they've locked the winch to hold the big sailboat in place. Two men are on deck, bailing. On the transom it says *Bluefin, Long Island, NY.*

I start over that way, but when the Reeses round the corner from Main Street I stop, go down on one knee, and pretend to tie my sneaker. I take my time, then straighten up and face the harbor. After a while I look over my shoulder. Mallory Reese is wearing white shorts, low-cut white sneakers, and a green MAINE sweatshirt. She's sort of sashaying, hair swinging back and forth, beside Charles Reese, who's got the old rich-boy walk going, one hand in his pocket, the other extended toward Erky, who's coming up from the dock. They shake and stand together, Erky bobbing his head, Reese jabbering and making little flipping motions with his free hand. Mallory says something and they stop and look at her. She says something else and walks off in my direction. Reese watches her go, then turns back to Erky. Mallory comes right up to me with a little grin on her face and says, "And just where were you this morning, you naughty boy?"

NINETEEN

"We waited *anxiously* for you." Mallory Reese says. She talks like a swank, but like she's making fun of herself at the same time, which is cool. She's got her hands in her pockets, pulling the shorts tight around her bottom, and her legs are goose-bumped from the breeze off the water. She's wearing these cat's-eye sunglasses that would probably look silly on somebody else. "Mr. Hartley was *dreadfully* put out," she says. "He *hates* it when things don't go as they're supposed to. Poor Mr. Hartley."

"I never said I'd do it," I say.

"That may be true," she says. "But I'm afraid your television career has suffered a severe blow."

"Oh well," I say.

She laughs and crosses her arms and looks back at the sailboat. I peek at her breasts, which are sort of *framed* by her arms, like she's holding a couple of fat little puppies. I swallow and look away. A flock of ducks paddles up by the float. I like the ducks. They come around for handouts every spring. I watch them for a while, then look back at Mallory. She's still staring over at the *Bluefin*.

"I hope it's not too bad," I say.

She turns her head, and her hair fans and settles on her shoulders. She smiles at me. "Oh, I suppose things are a little damp down below," she says. Then she lifts her sunglasses up and opens her eyes wide. "Oh my goodness," she says. "Did I really say that?" She covers her mouth with her fingertips.

I feel my goddamn face go red.

She laughs and pushes me. "I'm sure it's all your fault," she says.

"My fault?"

"Don't be modest," she says. "*Any*-way, according to Mr. Jura there was no structural damage. So we should be fine, once we're pumped out." She looks at me again with wide eyes.

I look at the ducks and wish I had some bread. Or Goldfish crackers. They love Goldfish. It would give me something to do. I can't think of anything else to do. The air has gotten thick as hell. I look sideways at Mallory, who's smiling out at the ducks. She's so goddamned nice, and then there's the wise-guy air that seems to say anything's possible. It all adds up on you.

She catches me staring, and laughs under her breath. She touches a finger to her lips. "Shall we try an experiment?" she says. "Walk down here with me, would you?"

"Down where?"

"Down here," she says, matter of factly. She starts off, and I follow her along the boardwalk, watching her legs, her bottom, her small, square shoulders. She walks off the end of the boardwalk to a little park with a flower garden, bench, a couple crabapple trees. There's a path that goes through it to the old footbridge across the river to the harbor park, and she follows the path until she's behind the first of the little trees. I can feel last year's crabapples under my feet. She faces me and my heart speeds up.

"Well?" she says. "Are you going to kiss me?"

"Kiss you?" I say.

"*You* know," she says. "Old human custom. You touch lips and sort of nibble around. It's fun if you've never tried it." Her eyebrows pop up over the top of her sunglasses, and she smiles with one corner of her mouth.

"What about your husband?" I say.

She moves closer and puts her hands on my arms. Then she shuts her eyes and makes it impossible for me *not* to kiss her. Her lips are soft, and I feel the tip of her tongue flicking my lips. I get a surge of energy and squeeze her against me and kiss her hard. She puts her hands on my chest and leans back in my arms. She pushes the sunglasses up on her head. Her eyes are bright, her cheeks are pink, and it's like she's shivering. I try to kiss her again, but she holds me off and forces a laugh. "My goodness," she says. Then she steps away and runs her hands through her hair. She tugs at her sweatshirt and clears her throat. "Good!" she says. "Are we ready?" And she starts around me. "Come along, Mr. Hull," she says.

I take her arm. "Wait, why did you do that?"

Her eyebrows go up. "Because I wanted to?" she says. She's got her usual amused look back, but she's still trembling.

"That's it?" I say.

She laughs and slides her sunglasses back into place. "I'm sorry," she says. "I've never kissed a handsome lobsterman before and I wanted to." She takes my hand and leads me out from behind the crabapple trees, over to the boardwalk. The sunlight feels warm, shining down across the tops of the buildings. We walk along the boardwalk, above the floats and the nosed-in, swamped dories and skiffs.

I say, "So do you always do what you want?"

"Doesn't everyone?" she says.

"What about your husband?"

"He certainly does what *he* wants!"

"That's not what I meant," I say.

She waves her other hand and laughs.

She lets go of my hand as we pass the parked cars to where I stopped to tie my shoelace. I see that Erky Jura and Charles Reese have moved down to the sailboat. The two men on board are still throwing fans of water over the side, the boat riding a bit higher. Erky has his hands on his hips, and nods his head while Reese talks. Then they shake hands. Erky goes back to his office and Reese walks toward Mallory and me. The collar is turned up on his white polo shirt and his mop of sandy hair bounces around as he walks. He's wearing sunglasses, too, and he frowns as he comes up to us.

"Hello, darling!" Mallory says. "We've been watching the ducks!"

"Have you?" Reese says. He looks at the ducks, circling in front of the boardwalk. He looks back at Mallory, then at me. He rocks on his feet and clears his throat.

"Too bad about the boat," I say.

"Yes, well, accidents will happen."

He shifts, like he's squaring himself up, and says, "So, Mr. Hartley was expecting you this morning."

"That's what I heard."

"He thought he had an agreement with you."

"I had to work."

"You were told we'd pay you," Reese says. Then he launches into a lecture about responsibility. He pulls a hand out of his pocket and opens it, like he's showing a dope something obvious. He talks real slow and leans on certain words: "Mr. Hartley *has* to be able to depend on the locals if he's going to continue to include them in his *broad*casts. It caused us *innumerable* problems when you weren't there as expected. We were lucky to be able to salvage the *show*."

"I never said I'd be there."

"It was *understood*, for God's sake."

I'm about to tell him what to do with his lecture, but just then Eddy Cranberry shuffles around the corner, and I get a better idea.

Eddy pokes along with his head down, mumbling away with the usual bottle of juice in his hand. He doesn't even know we're there. He swings over to pick up the debris, bending and scooping the garbage into the can, sort of hunching along with his arms on his thighs, the overalls stretched across his big butt. He makes short work of it, takes a big gulp of juice, and lets out a belch. Then he makes his way down the gangway to the float. He still hasn't noticed us—he generally doesn't notice tourists anyway, and Reese is between me and him.

Reese is still lecturing me. The guy can *talk*. He tells me that the local broadcasts are a *cooperative venture*. If you take a *portion* away, he explains, it affects the *whole*.

I see Eddy tugging on one of the skiffs, trying to work it up onto the float. The skiff is filled with water, and he's putting his back into it, the cords standing out on his neck. He grunts, moves the skiff a foot—a foot more than a normal human being could move it. He can't tip it yet, though. In the background I hear Reese telling me that despite it all, Hartley has a very forgiving nature, and if I were to go over to the marina and apologize, I just might get a second chance.

I raise a hand and say, "Hold that thought."

Reese shuts his mouth in mid-sentence. He doesn't look very happy about it. I step to the side and call down to Eddy. He looks up at me and smiles without letting go of the skiff. His arms are like a gorilla's, long and thick with muscle.

"Come on up and say hello!" I say.

Reese crosses his arms and Mallory looks at me over the top of her sunglasses. Eddy lifts the skiff's bow a couple of inches so it won't scrape and walks it back. He lets it go, grabs his juice, and comes up the gangway. He marches along the boardwalk, spanking the tin top of each piling with his free hand. When he gets within fifty feet, Mallory says, "My goodness!"

"Hey!" Eddy says, walking up.

Reese backs away, looking disgusted.

"Local color!" I explain.

Reese takes Mallory's arm and pulls her away without another word. They go off across the lot and up Ferry Street toward the square. Mallory looks back, but Reese puts a hand on her neck and steers her onto Main Street. They walk in stride around the corner.

"Hey?" Eddy says.

"Never mind, buddy," I say. "Go ahead and finish your job."

Eddy heads back to the float. He grabs the skiff and lifts its bow. I walk over to look at the *Bluefin*. Erky's boys are working a big vacuum pump down over the cabin steps. I watch them wrestle with it, then I continue on down the wharf. None of the shops is busy. The sun is behind the other side of town now, and shadows fall across Seaview Street and it's cooling off. The air is still scrubbed clean, though, and I feel pretty good walking up the hill, thinking, "Hey Reese, your wife just slapped the make on me!" But then I have to laugh.

"Oh, you're a big stud, all right," I say to myself.

Halfway home I see somebody bouncing down the hill in a pickup, two guys actually, laughing at something, and that reminds me that my own truck is still in the parking lot at the landing. I wonder if I can get away with leaving it there, but then turn around and head back. They'll ticket you if you have local plates.

TWENTY

That night I stand on the deck smoking a cigarette and it seems like a million stars have crowded overhead. There's only a shaving of moon and the sky is extra black, so the stars really stand out. I've been outside for a while, wondering what to do with myself. I think about calling Niki, but can't decide if that's a good idea or if it might just be using her. I try to imagine us getting it on to see if I can believe it. But I can't see it very clear. I try thinking about Mallory Reese instead, and that's better, but I still can't see it all the way through.

I'm such a godforsaken idiot sometimes.

I blow smoke at the sky and watch an airplane pass overhead, running lights blinking. That's the way to do it. Stay above the damn fog and everything else. I polish off my beer and wonder how many are left in the shed. Then I drop the butt into the beer can and set the can down. I walk down the steps and over to the driveway and lean over the pickup's seat to grab the old basketball out of the extended cab. I throw a few bank shots into the hoop bolted to the peak of the shed, moving up close, catching the ball on one bounce, flipping it up and off the backboard and through the hoop, catching it again, flipping it again. It's something I do when I can't think of anything else. Ever since I was five or six years old. After a while I toss the ball back into the truck and trot into the house. I find Niki's number and call. It rings four times, and her voice says, "Hi!" I'm halfway into my spiel before I realize it's her answering machine and she's saying, "I'm sorry I'm not here to take your call, but please leave me a message and I'll call you back *wicked soon!*"

I hang up, relieved in a chickenshit sort of way.

I go back outside and cross the lawn to the tall ash trees—brittle trees that dropped a lot of branches in the storm. I lean against the one that supports a side of my rope hammock and remember the deer carcasses the old man hung from this same tree. Polky used one for a punching bag once, and I picture him swatting it like *Rocky* in the meat locker. I see Niki running off with her hand over her mouth, and Bobby Lawson laughing and skip-scuffing in the grass. I remember my folks watching from the porch, coffee cups in their hands, my old man just shaking his head.

I look at the black water, see pieces of the crescent moon. Downstream a motorcycle sputters across the bridge and winds off past the point on the other side, following Seaview as it hooks around the harbor, extending down the peninsula without ever connecting to any points inland. There's an old movie star living down there, the president of a credit card company, several retired CIA guys, or so rumor has it. There are some old ramshackle homes, too, falling in on themselves. It used to be more of a community, with a little store and restaurant down on the water. But they've been closed for a couple years now. Somebody bought the land but hasn't done anything with it yet.

I walk upstream, past sumacs, the big willow, and a couple of small birches, then three different kinds of spruce. I walk past the bog and down another path to where my skiff sits on the dock. I perch on the skiff and look downstream again. A car crosses the bridge and I see its headlights lighting up the birches on the other side. I look at my watch. It's only nine o'clock, so I think maybe I'll go down to Cobb's for a beer, see if there are any loose women around. I'm getting a little worked up to try my luck. I light up a cigarette and think about that. Then I pitch the butt into the creek and walk back to the house. I still want to go and see who's at Cobb's, but sitting still has made me lazy. I go into the house to think about it and the phone rings—Polky.

"Hey!" he says, "What the fuck are you doing?"

"Not much. Was that you I saw go by?"

"Yeah, I'm on the old payphone at the store. I had to meet a guy down here to make some plans. I'll tell you all about it soon as you join the team."

"Whatever," I say.

Polky laughs. "That ain't why I called, anyway. I called to tell you I saw your best friend Danny Brinker coming out of the steak house with Trace White and the Zeagull. Came out and hopped right into White's Jaguar. One big happy family. I blasted right by them and Danny looked at me like he'd seen a ghost."

"Really?"

"Yeah, really."

"So you think he's the one?"

"He looked pretty fucking guilty."

"He's been hanging around that crowd."

"Exactly."

"Why would he do it, though?"

"Maybe they've got some paper on him, too. Maybe he always wanted to be a swank when he grew up. Who the fuck knows?" He cusses me one more time and tells me to get my head out of my ass. Then he hangs up the phone. I have a beer on the deck and think it over. Then I jog down the steps and over to the pickup. I'll go down to Cobb's, but more to mull over what I've just heard than to look for a girl. I drive down to the five-way. The sidewalks are pretty empty, just a few guys standing under a streetlight, and two girls walking stiffly up the other side toward the Lord Pequot, like they think the guys are watching them, which they are.

All the brick buildings are dark except for nightlights.

I turn down to the landing and park. I get out and break the filter off a cigarette, lighting the frayed end and smoking it like a joint so I can get a good burn. I look across the harbor at the marina, listen to the skiffs jostling at the float, the couplings clanging. The blue sailboat is still tied up in front of Erky's. I take another drag on the cigarette and it makes me woozy.

That's when the cruiser comes down from the square and pulls into the space beside my pickup. There are two police officers inside, a young guy—new, I guess—and Chief Lazaro. Lazaro gets out and heaves the door shut in slow-motion, like John Wayne. It makes me want to laugh. He stands there with his hands on his gunbelt. I've known him for twenty years, since he used to volunteer at Booster's Club basketball on Saturday mornings. He was all right back then.

"Mr. Hull," Lazaro says.

"Chief." I lean back against the hood.

"Fine evening," the chief says. He walks onto the boardwalk and stands there with both hands on his wide belt. He's got this silly Special Forces–style beret on that somebody thought would be a good idea. He stands there like he's staring out to sea, then turns all at once and says, "That you I saw cutting through the five-way the other night?"

"I go through there sometimes." I drop the last pinch of my cigarette and rub it out with my boot.

"Wrong answer," Lazaro says.

"What do you want me to say?"

"How about the truth?"

"The truth is I go through there a lot."

Lazaro walks toward me like a tough guy. He comes right up close and looks into my eyes. I resist the urge to knock the beret off his head.

"Now you listen," the chief says, "and listen good. Next time you see me coming, you pull over and stop. You dodge me again and by God you'll wish you hadn't."

"I don't remember seeing any lights."

"Lights or no, you pull over and stop." Lazaro stares at me, then turns around and swaggers back to the cruiser. He poses there again, looking across the roof at me. Then he snatches the door open and slides inside. The cruiser backs around with the young cop staring out the window and takes off up Ferry Street, squeaking around the corner onto Main.

I stuff my hands into my pockets and head across the parking lot. I walk up Ferry Street, hang a right on the brick sidewalk, and look through Cobb's front window, but don't see any loose women in there. Maybe they'll come in later though. You never quite know with loose women.

TWENTY-ONE

I've been sitting at the bar for an hour, sipping pints, thinking about what Polky told me, and I keep thinking it just might be Danny Brinker who dropped the dime on me. I try not to commit totally to the idea. I could still be wrong.

As far as my other concern goes, I've pretty much given up on getting lucky. Even Molly, who seemed like a possibility, isn't going to be the answer. She's got someone lined up already, a skinny young guy sitting at the other end of the bar, watching her like a fish hawk.

I finish my beer, look at the foamy glass. Then I dig in my pocket for some cash, but while I'm still thumbing through the bills the door to the street opens and in walks old Danny Brinker himself. He hesitates when he sees me, but then catches my eye in the mirror and comes on over in his rocking, bow-legged walk. I've seen him walk like this since he was eight or nine years old, and it makes me sad to remember him as a kid.

"Hey man," he says, "we missed you this morning." He puts his hands on the bar and sort of vaults onto the stool, like the Lone Ranger jumping onto Silver.

"That so?" I say.

"Yeah, old Hartley was a little steamed."

"Fuck Hartley," I say.

Danny laughs. It sounds a little nervous to me. "*Somebody's* in a good mood," he says.

"Fuck you, too," I say, but my heart's not really in it.

Molly pours two beers and brings them over. "You all right, hon?" she says to me.

My glass goes frosty in the warm room. "Finest kind," I say.

Danny and I are the only ones at the bar, except for Molly's boyfriend. The ball game is tuned in on the wall TV and a few local boys are watching from the booths. I grab a handful of beer nuts and shake them into my mouth one at a time, telling myself to be cool.

"So, you get caught in that squall?" Danny says after a while.

"A little bit," I say.

"I see the hotshots did." Danny points with his thumb toward the landing. "Pretty wild out there, huh?"

"I guess so," I say, and look up at the baseball game: the Sox have a lefty pitching who isn't fooling anybody. One pitch later he's walking to the dugout and the manager is standing on the mound waiting with the ball. The relief pitcher jogs in, takes his time throwing warm-ups, the game resumes and the first batter hits a rope over the center fielder's head into the triangle.

"So you heard about Polky, right?" Danny says then.

I watch the runner slide into third. "What about him?"

"That they used him when you didn't show up?"

It takes me a second. Then I look at him. "You're kidding."

"Nope," Danny says.

"Whose idea was *that*?"

"Hartley's!" Danny says. "He reamed old Dickweed a new one for not having you there. Told him he'd better find somebody pronto, and there was Polky. Hartley talked to him for a minute or two, and they went ahead and put him on. He might go back on tomorrow."

Danny goes on about Polky's TV appearance, and while I'm listening to him something drifts into my mind. I nod for Danny's benefit while I ponder it. I can't see that I'll be any worse off if it doesn't pan out. I look at him like I'm distracted and then I let my eyes focus and I say, "So how long was he on?"

"Oh, four or five minutes," Danny says.

"Was he nervous?"

"Are you kidding? He kept calling Hartley *Chummy*."

That makes me laugh for real. But then I go back into my act. I let him see the wheels turning. Then I say, "He's on again in the morning?"

"That's what they're thinking."

Now I try to look disappointed.

"What?" Danny says. "You want your job back?"

"Naw, I just wish I could watch . . . " I move my hand like I'm chopping the sentence off, give him this lame grin, look up at the TV. I can feel him watching me, but I keep my eyes on the game. The Sox have brought in another pitcher who's throwing his warm-ups. I like the way he gives a flip with his glove to tell the catcher what's coming, then rocks into his windup. When Danny starts in about Polky again, I check my watch and slide off my seat.

"Out of here?" he says.

"Places to go," I say, but I stop on the way out and beckon Molly down to the end of the bar. "I need a favor," I say in a normal voice. I don't care if Danny hears this part.

"Sure, hon," Molly says.

I lean close and whisper, "After I leave, let Danny know you think I'm going on a run of some kind tonight. Tell him you're worried about me lately." I peek over her shoulder and see Danny watching.

"What are you up to?" Molly whispers back.

"I'll tell you later. Give me a bottle of Captain Morgan's, and when Danny asks what's up, tell him you think I wanted it for a trip."

She looks at me, thinking it over. But then she ducks down and hands me the bottle of Morgan's. I give her some money and tuck the bottle under my jacket. I give Danny a little salute. He waves back without changing his expression.

I get my pickup and head out of town along Route One on the Rockland bypass to Owls Head—all part of my brainstorm. I drive to the dirt road and park at the dead end. Then I walk through the bushes to Bobby Lawson's cabin. It's clear out, the stars bright, and that little moon hanging over the cove. There are lights on in the cabin and I can smell the smoke from its chimney. It smells like he's burning scrap pine. I step across the hole in the porch and tap on the door. Nothing happens, and I tap again, and this time Susan Lawson opens the door a crack.

"Can I speak to Bobby?" I say.

"He ain't here," Susan says.

"Just ask him if I can see him for a minute."

She's wearing an old bathrobe, holding it shut with one hand, and chewing on her lip so that her little bottom teeth show. She's got teeth like pale kernels of corn.

"I want to apologize for the other night," I say. "I was wrong."

"Yes, you was!" Susan says.

"I admit it," I say. "Ask Bobby if he'll talk to me."

Bobby himself steps out from behind the door. "Sorry, Troy. I didn't know whether you was out for bear or not. You want to come in?"

I look past him into the foyer. "I don't want to wake up your kids."

"They're good sleepers."

"Can we just talk outside?"

Bobby squints at me. Then he gives his wife a pat on the shoulder. "I'll be right back, hon," he says, and comes out onto the porch, pulling the door shut behind him. Bobby's wearing sweatpants and a hoodie and a Red Sox cap. He pulls a pack of Camels out of the hand-warmer pocket and offers one. I take it and light it on Bobby's match. Bobby ducks his head, lights his own, shakes the match out. "So what's up?" he says.

"I think I know who ratted me out," I say.

"It wasn't me."

"I believe you," I say, "But I want to make *sure* it couldn't be you, no offense. See, I think I've got them set up. I'm going to take a run out somewhere and see if they drop the dime on me. If they do, and you're with me, that means it's who I think it is. I'll give you fifty bucks for your time."

"So who's the culprit?" Bobby says with a funny smile, like he's proud for using a word I wouldn't expect.

"I shouldn't say, in case I'm wrong again."

"Good idea," he says. He frowns like he's thinking it over. Then he says, "I guess I'll go with you. Then you'll know it wasn't me. Just lemme tell the old lady." He opens the door and says, "Me and Troy got an errand to do. Don't wait up, hon." He shuts the door.

We walk across the two-by-eights to the cove and head off through the bushes. It's dark enough that you have to be careful not to take a branch in the eye. We come out to the pickup and Bobby yanks the door open and climbs in. I get in the other side.

"What have we got here?" Bobby holds up the Captain Morgan's, looks at it like it's gold.

"Not now," I say. "You can have it when we get back."

"Sweet!"

On the way to Pequot, Bobby smokes too much even for *me*. I crack my window, keeping an eye out for Lazaro. We go through the light, which is blinking yellow, and at the square I turn back along Seaview Street and climb the hill.

"Too bad about Charlie's house," Bobby says.

"Yeah." I pull the truck into the driveway. "I'll go fill my thermos," I say, and I run in and nuke up some coffee. I grab some chips and Slim Jims, too. Then I go back out. We walk down the path to the dock. I hold the skiff until Bobby's in—he takes the rear thwart—then step in myself. A cloud has moved over the moon, and it's even darker out. The cloud is frosted faintly by moonlight. I push off with an oar and start downstream toward the bridge. The little moon comes back out and breaks up on the water. I row us around the bend, wondering if I'm doing something useless.

"Nice spot you got here, Troy," Bobby says.

"It stays pretty much the same."

"That's what's good about it."

We float under the bridge and I think about Zeiglaar and White and Danny. It bums me out as much as before. I row us across the harbor. With two in the skiff, we ride pretty low past leaves and branches left by the storm. Ahead I can see Danny's yard lights. At the *Julie Marie*, Bobby scissors over the side and I pull to the mooring to swap out. I climb onto the foredeck and make my way back. Before I drop down I look across the wheelhouse roof at the marina. From up here I can see there's a light on in Danny's office. I grab the roof and swing down behind the wheel.

"All a-*board*!" Bobby says, and laughs.

I start the engine and throw her in gear.

TWENTY-TWO

"So where we heading?" Bobby sits on the engine hatch, smoking a cigarette. He's got his cap low on his forehead, and all I can see of his face is his chin. "What's the plan, cap'n?" he says.

"Well, I want to look suspicious," I say.

Smoke leaks from under the brim of his cap. "How are you fixing to do that?"

"I don't know, exactly."

We putt up to the island. I wonder about running lights. I want to make sure Danny doesn't miss us, but a smuggler would probably leave them off, so that's what I do.

"How about Big Branch?" Bobby says. "We could run out there, look like we're up to no good."

It's not a bad idea. Big Branch has been an outlaw way station for a long time, and the clam cops know it. And it's a two-and-a-half-hour ride, out and back, which will be enough time for anything that might happen.

"I like it," I say.

Bobby sits up a little straighter.

We ease past the island into the bay and I lean out, watching until the ledge slips past, and then I give her the gas and turn south, toward Big Branch. I look at Bobby and raise my voice over the engine. "You want to pour some coffee?"

He picks over the cups on the dashboard and makes a face. He leaves the wheelhouse, rinses them with the salt-water hose, brings them back, and fills them from the thermos. I point at the bag of junk food, and Bobby grabs a Slim Jim for himself and a bag of potato chips for me. He tears the Slim Jim open with his teeth and takes a bite. I rip the bag of chips open and eat the whole thing in a few bites. It's mostly air, as usual. There's enough starlight to see the Havens: black and hilly, ten miles out.

"She rides nice," Bobby says. "I like a wood boat."

"Uh-huh," I say.

"Mine's wood, too, such as it is."

"I saw it up in your yard."

"She's got a few problems."

"Don't we all," I say.

We move over long swells left over from the storm. It's like the bay is rolling us out toward Big Branch on its own. I think about all the water in the bay. Off to the right on the mainland I can see village lights, a glow over the bigger towns.

"So what've you been up to?" Bobby says after a while.

"Not much."

"I'm still clamming," he says.

"Yeah?" I say.

"Got to keep food on the table."

"Making any money?"

"I'm hoping it'll pick up."

"I've heard there was money in it."

"Yup, when things fall right."

"Hard work though."

"I ain't afraid to work." He's got another cigarette going, and he's pushed his baseball cap back on his head. He sees me smiling and says, "What's so funny?"

I never could help teasing Bobby. In school everybody teased him. He was a little guy with a shitty haircut, who wasn't any good at sports or schoolwork or anything else that really counted. I used to feel guilty sometimes about it.

"Bobby," I say, "when in your life did you ever have a real job?"

"When did you?" he says right back.

"Lobstering's a real job."

"Naw, it ain't. Lobstering's what you do because your old man done it and his old man done it and so on and so forth. A *job's* working for somebody else. Punching a time clock. Nine to five bullshit." He holds the cigarette like a dart and points it at me. "I'd fish if I could," he says. "I didn't have no trouble fishing while you was away. I done all right, too. But then you came home and that was the end of that."

"Excuse me all to hell," I say.

"I ain't *blaming* you."

"You shouldn't."

"I'm not. You shouldn't have blamed me either. Nobody else was using that water."

"How about when I came back?"

"I didn't know you was going to start in. I thought you'd go back to school. All you had to do was set your traps. I'd've pulled mine. You could've had it back without fighting about it."

"You should have said so."

"Like you'd listen to me."

I change course a few degrees. Big Branch swings like a dark blot across the bow, still miles off, though.

"None of you ever paid attention to what a Lawson said anyways," he says.

"Oh, here we go," I say.

"It's the goddamn truth."

I look at him. "We talking high school now?"

"High school, junior high, grammar school."

"You used to come up to the creek."

"Yeah, some," Bobby says. "But I got picked on just as bad there."

Something breaks the surface off to starboard and disappears. I watch, but it doesn't show again. Probably a seal. But maybe not. You never know what else might be cruising around below. I turn back to the wheel. "Everybody gets teased," I say.

Bobby just snorts at that. Then he leans out and throws his cigarette overboard. He dips into the bag for another Slim Jim. "You mind if I eat these up?" he says.

"Go for it."

He tears the wrapper off, takes a bite. We steam along and he doesn't say anything.

"All right," I say. "Maybe you got teased more."

"Let me ask you," Bobby says. "Did Bill Polky ever dunk *your* head in the toilet?"

"No." I can't help laughing.

"Did Ziggy Campbell ever set fire to your homework? Homework you had done on time for once in your fricking life?"

"I kind of remember that."

"We was eating lunch out in the grove behind the school. And Carla Swenson—that snooty bitch!—distracted me while Ziggy torched my lunch. My homework was inside and I got a week's detention out of it." He takes another bite of the Slim Jim. "I *wondered* why the hell Carla was talking to me."

"The teacher blamed you?"

"What do you think? She said I shouldn't carry homework in my lunch bag anyways, because it got all wrinkled up and stained when I did."

"What happened to Ziggy?"

"Same as me, like it was both our faults."

We ride along. It's so dark and clear out on the water, it's almost scary. For a minute or two I almost want to turn around. But the hell with that, I think then. You've gone this far.

"You remember Booster's Club?" Bobby says.

"Sure."

"You remember me coming in eighth grade?"

"Maybe," I say.

"You all taped me up with ankle tape and pulled my pants down and stuck me in a locker with a jockstrap over my face, remember?

The cheerleaders were practicing and you guys brought them in to take a look. You must remember that."

I'm trying not to laugh. "Yeah," I say.

"I had a *real* good start in high school after that." Bobby says. "I could play ball, too, I was fast as hell," he says. "If you guys hadn't ruint it for me I coulda played in high school, probably. Or maybe run track or something."

"I remember you could run pretty fast," I say.

"Not fast enough, though." He swallows and laughs. "Screw it," he says. "Gimme another one of them Slim Jims." He reaches into the bag and takes one out and a bag of chips.

Within the hour Big Branch is looming out of the darkness. The harbor is on the north side of the island, sheltered by points that reach out like two arms. I run the *Julie Marie* straight in and up to the old steamboat dock. Bobby scampers out, I toss him the lines, and he snaps them around the cleats like a rodeo star tying up a calf. I check my watch, look up at the island. "Want to stretch your legs?"

"Okay," he says.

We climb the ladder to the pier. There's a shack and the dock and that's it. A stack of traps on the end of the dock. Tall pine trees all around, and a dirt road leading into the woods. It's two in the morning, the island almost totally dark. There's no real village on Big Branch anyway, just a few houses spaced around the island. We walk down a skinny washboard road and up a slope to a crossing with the little post office and the local church. The church has a tall white steeple. Bobby gives me a cigarette and lights one for himself. We walk through the crossing and the pines crowd up close again and something rustles away into the woods.

Bobby says, "Fox."

"Uh-huh."

"Or coyote," he says, pronouncing it ki-yoat.

"Maybe."

We walk on into the island. It's about two miles long and a mile wide, with plenty of woods. We go by a dark house with traps and buoys piled in the yard and a pickup parked in the dirt driveway. When we pass the old Grange Hall somebody comes out of the bushes and walks down the hill toward us. In the faint moonlight I can see that he's holding his right arm straight down against his leg.

"Hold on, there," the guy says.

We pull up and wait. A big beefy guy comes down to the road. There's definitely a pistol in his hand, but he's pointing it at the ground.

"Jesus, Willie," Bobby says, "don't shoot us, okay?"

"Who's that?" The big guy peers at us. "Bobby L.?"

"Yes!" Bobby says. "So don't shoot me."

"What the hell are you doing out here at two in the morning?"

"Me and Troy, we just come out for a ride."

"Troy who?"

"Troy Hull," I say. I've never talked to Willie Loomis, but I've seen him ashore and heard plenty of stories about him. There are a lot of Loomises on Big Branch, and Willie's supposed to be one of the meanest.

"Troy *Hull*?" Loomis says. "Did I know your old man?"

"Chances are."

"He weren't a bad guy, for a mainlander."

"He always spoke well of you," I say.

Loomis belly-laughs. Then he thumbs the safety on his pistol and tucks it into his waistband. He's about six-four and probably goes two-seventy-five or so. A typical Big Brancher. But I guess he's decided not to shoot us, which is good. He looks at me and says, "You played a little basketball too, didn't you?"

"A little."

"Bunch of us went to the States to watch you guys play. I 'member they called you *Troy Terrific* in the paper."

"That's right!" Bobby says. "I forgot that!"

"Go ahead and forget it again," I say.

Loomis chuckles. "So what are you ladies *really* up to?"

Bobby looks at me.

"Somebody ratted me out," I say. "We took a pretend run to set them up so I could see if it's who I think it is."

"Ratted you out for what?" Loomis looks me up and down. "You been peeing over the side?"

"Not much worse," I say.

"What?"

"A warp run."

"Jesus Christ!" Loomis makes wide eyes.

Bobby and I laugh.

"Well, I wouldn't prowl around too much this time of night," Loomis says. "Some fool killed Ralph P's dog a month ago for getting into his chickens and Ralph killed somebody else's dog to make up for it and it went on from there and now you don't know who the hell might be sneaking around looking for trouble." He peers into the bushes, like he's just remembered that *he's* out in the middle of the night, too.

"We were just stretching our legs," Bobby says.

"You ain't looking for work, are you Bobby?"

"No, sir," Bobby says. "I'm a clam-digger now."

"Well, you let me know if you change your mind. I ain't found anybody worth a damn since you quit. You know they come and go like the fucking moon."

Bobby gives me a look.

Loomis takes the gun out and salutes with it, then crosses the road and sort of melts back into the bushes. We hear him moving away, but he's pretty quiet for a big guy.

On the walk back Bobby says, "I stern-manned out here for a year or so for Willie. Well, for all the Loomises. There's five of 'em, and they sorta passed me around, depending on who was short-handed. I was second man, third man. There's pretty good money in it. They haul a lot of lobster out here. But it was too damn hard getting back and forth. I used to take the mail plane, but that got pretty expensive, and then it'd fog in and I'd be stranded."

As we walk, Bobby swings his arms like a soldier. We pass the church and turn down to the dock. I can't believe how quiet it is. Even in Pequot you're liable to hear a car or two, no matter what time it is. But there's nothing out here this time of night, except for Willie Loomis and Ralph P. and whoever else is slinking around.

"Got the lines," Bobby says.

I climb aboard, Bobby throws the lines in and joins me. I start the engine and we run out between the points. As soon as we're clear I see the mainland lights in the distance. They look as far away as the stars, but they're multi-colored. We head back, drinking coffee and eating potato chips, talking about high school and old teachers and basketball games. We're not halfway back when we see the clam cops. I guess they were running without their lights, and after they detected us they waited until they were close. Their spotlight comes on, too, and they start broadcasting about boarding us for a routine inspection. I take the power out and watch them come chugging up.

"Bingo," Bobby says.

TWENTY-THREE

The Marine Patrol boat swings along broadside, her wake rocking us and the spotlight sweeping the choppy surface to see if we've dumped anything. Then it comes up into my face. I turn away and rub my eyes. Rope thumps on the deck, and Officer Tracy Thibeault yells, "Take the lines, make the two boats fast!"

"Who the hell's that?" Bobby says.

"The new girl."

"Oh, shit," he says.

We take the lines and pull the clam cops close, then, when the boats are snugged up tight, we cinch the lines. I hear the fenders rubbing, like someone making a balloon squeak. The boats are almost the same size: theirs is a confiscated lobster boat painted all white and jazzed up with a big engine and radar and all the standard cop gear, renamed *Vigilant*.

Don Moody steps from the *Vigilant* up onto the *Julie Marie*'s rail and turns sideways to drop down onto the deck. He staggers a little as the boats shift. Then he says, "Good evening, gentlemen."

The spotlight comes back up into the boat.

I hold a hand up. "Can you shut that thing off?"

"Cut the spot!" Moody says. After a second the light goes out. I see that Moody hasn't shaved or even combed his hair: his normal pompadour is all messed up. Even his handlebar looks a bit ragged. He must have been sound asleep when they rousted him.

Officer Thibeault leans over the joined rails and shines a flashlight into my boat, holding it like a fat little spear, flicking the beam here and there.

"So!" Don Moody says.

"So, you got nothing better to do?" I say.

"Apparently not," Moody says, and it seems he's already a little doubtful. He looks at Bobby Lawson and says, "What are you doing here, Bobby?"

Bobby holds his palms up. "Nothing."

"Nothing," Don Moody says. He rocks up on his toes and back to his heels. "I suppose he's an improvement over Polky, Troy, but I don't know how much."

"Careful, you'll hurt his feelings."

"That I doubt."

"Are you going to search them?" Tracy Thibeault says. She's still leaning on her elbows, aiming the flashlight around.

Moody looks over his shoulder and says, "Everything's under control."

"I see you lucked out again," I say.

The flashlight beam hits me in the face, and hangs there before dropping away. Moody closes an eye and looks at me long enough to show he might agree, even if he can't say it out loud. Then he says, "I suppose since I'm here I should take a look around, with your permission."

"Go for it," I say.

Moody's got a trooper flashlight too, one of those long metal ones that doubles as a club, and he shines it around the wheelhouse and then squeezes through the little door into the cuddy. He bangs around below for a while, going through the motions, but he's figured out that I'm in the clear again. He rejoins us and looks into the chart compartment. He shuts that little door and works his way around the wheelhouse. Then finally he walks aft, where Bobby and I stand with our hands in our pockets.

"Officer Moody?" Tracy Thibeault calls over.

"They seem to be clean," Moody calls back.

"Maybe we should tow them in to dry dock!"

"No reason to," Moody says.

"You can't search a boat with a flashlight!"

I laugh and the flashlight beam hits my face again. I grin right into it. Moody raises his voice and says, "We got no probable cause. And knock it off with the flashlight."

Thibeault moves the beam away.

Moody looks back at me. "I don't suppose you'd care to tell me just what the hell is going on?"

"Just out for a ride," I say. "Bobby here's thinking of stern-manning with me. Just getting him used to the boat. We were up, and it was nice out."

"If you're playing games . . . "

"Not with you," I say.

Moody twiddles his mustache, makes a face, and turns away. He puts a foot on the *Julie Marie*'s rail, bounces on his other foot, and heaves up and over onto the *Vigilant*. I hear him say something to Tracy Thibeault, and then he looks back at us and calls, "You can throw that first line back. Wait'll we separate a little before you give us the second one."

"Aye, aye!" Bobby says. He whips the forward line free, snakes it onto the *Vigilant*. He loosens the other and angles it taut around the cleat until they've turned away. Then he tosses it aboard the Marine Patrol boat. "Have a good evening!" he yells as they power up. He comes back into the wheelhouse and says, "I love it! This is like when a cop pulls you over and you ain't started drinking yet!"

I start the engine and we head off toward the mainland. The bay lies flat and dark around us. The moon has gone down and the stars crowd close above.

"I guess somebody's been keeping an eye on you, all right," Bobby says.

"Looks that way."

"What are you going to do about it?"

"I don't know yet."

"Who is it?"

"Danny Brinker," I say after a second.

"No shit?" Bobby says.

"I wouldn't have believed it, either."

I head for the beacon at the end of the breakwater. After a while I angle toward Owls Head Light. There are still plenty of other lights along the shore, even this late.

"Well," Bobby says, "I'm glad I could help."

I laugh, pull out my wallet, fork over two twenties and a ten.

"Thank you kindly," he says.

"No problem," I say.

We ride on back to Owls Head, passing a tall, clanging bell buoy. I watch the lights come closer, the dark, hilly mainland push the stars higher. The tide is going out, so I have to be careful. I reverse the engine and bring the stern in, then hold her steady while Bobby jumps onto his decrepit old dock.

"Well, good night," he says.

I look around at the lighter swatch of Ash Point Beach to our left. "How much land have you got here?" I ask him.

"Almost ten acres."

"That's not bad."

"Used to be a couple thousand, back in the day."

"At least you got to keep the best part."

"For now," Bobby says.

"Yeah. Well, goodnight," I say. Then I remember, grab the bottle of rum, and toss it to him.

Bobby leans over to push the boat free of the dock, and I head for home in the dark.

TWENTY-FOUR

It's seven-thirty, and I've already thrown on jeans and flannel shirt and gone downstairs for breakfast when my head clears and I remember Big Branch, Bobby Lawson, and Danny Brinker. I slow down, pour coffee, sit at the table to decide about hauling. I'm tired and my eyes hurt and I feel like going back to bed, but once I'm up and dressed that never works. So I take my cereal and a glass of OJ into the living room and switch on the TV to check out *American Road.* I'm looking for Polky, but instead I get a head shot of Donald Hartley, showing his horsy teeth. Then the camera backs away and I see Keith Zeiglaar sitting with Hartley, so I guess a repeat performance by Polky is not in the cards today. Maybe Hartley didn't want someone calling him *Chummy* again. He and Zeiglaar are both wearing sunglasses and you can see sailboats in the background, all the tall masts.

"We're going to pan around the harbor of *Pay-cot*, Maine," Hartley says, "and Mr. Keith Zeiglaar, out-*standing* member of the Pequot Chamber of Commerce, is going to describe just what we're looking at. Keith?"

"Hide your French fries!" I yell at the TV.

Keith nudges his sunglasses and smiles. The camera pans around at trees, steeples, the mountain, and the harbor while he gives a rundown of the area and tells everyone how it's become a regular *Mecca* for vacationers. They show the schooner and Keith talks about how they sail for a week at a time with folks from Nebraska and Wyoming who've never seen the ocean, and how the crew turns them into real sea-dogs, hauling anchor and working lines, and how they have lobster bakes on island beaches in the dark.

"Fantastic!" Hartley says. "How do I get on one of those trips?"

"You just stop in to the chamber," Keith says. "Pick up a brochure. Or you can call our toll-free number." They put the number on the screen, while the camera holds on the schooner. Then they show the old stone tower on top of Burnt Mountain, and Keith talks about the hotel that used to be up there, and the poet's plaque, and a little about her childhood in Pequot.

I take my bowl into the kitchen and grab some coffee. Back in the living room they're showing this rich-guy farm from down the peninsula, and its belted Galloway cows behind a split-rail fence. I remember the guy who owns the farm managed to get a break on his taxes with some kind of deal that guarantees common people the right to walk by and look at it.

Hartley says he'll be broadcasting from *Pay-cot* for the whole rest of the week, and that he just can't wait to share more of *spectacular Midcoast Maine* with his viewers. Then they go to a commercial.

I switch the TV off and finish my coffee. I put the cup in the sink and go outside. Down by the water I spook a fish hawk out of a tree on the opposite bank. He drops into a glide, then powers on up the creek past three bird-shit-covered boulders bulking out of the water. A shag stands on one of the boulders, wings out, looking like a hood ornament. All the other shags are dunking for fish, popping back up, and swallowing with their skinny bills waving up at the sky. The creek is splashy with alewives, and sunlight breaks up off the water. It's pretty nice. But I have to get going. I slide the skiff into the water, then hold it close to the dock and step in. I seat the oars and head on down the creek. All the shags take off, making the usual racket. The seagulls shriek and spin through the air. Some of the shags fly under the bridge, and others pop up over it, and on the other side they join back together and mass off across the harbor. I follow in the skiff. I've decided to go see my pal Danny Brinker. Not that I know what will happen when I get there. Maybe I'll just cold-cock the little son-of-a-bitch.

The current takes me under the old iron bridge. I angle toward the *Julie Marie*, liking the low sweep from wheelhouse to stern. I think it's a lot prettier than the blue sailboat riding high, a hundred feet away. They've moved her closer to Danny's and she's moored to the bow now. I smile to see it, and the words *damp down below* ring in my mind, and then, like I've conjured her, Mallory Reese comes out of the cabin in little white shorts and a striped jersey. I hold the oars still and watch her swoop around the cockpit, picking up plastic cups and paper plates. It looks like they had a party last night to celebrate the return of their boat. She moves up to the stern, turns with her arms full, sees me, and stops. Then she hugs all the party debris with one arm and waves with the other. Somehow she manages to be graceful the whole while.

"Ahoy!" she says.

I pat the water with the oars, pull up close. "Morning," I say. I'm a little in awe of the way she looks, standing there hip-cocked in the sunlight.

"Are you going out?" she says.

"I was heading over to see Danny."

"I'm afraid you're out of luck," Mallory says. She nods toward the landing, where there's a small crowd gathered on the boardwalk, a few more down on the float. "He and my dear husband are working with the TV stars this morning. Mr. Hartley wants absolutely *everyone* there to make sure it goes properly." She smiles. "As you know, there were a few glitches with yesterday's broadcast."

I dip the oars to hold the skiff steady.

"Missing guest stars, for example," she continues.

"I heard he got by all right."

"Oh yes, he was lucky."

I laugh, thinking about Polky. "In more ways than one."

She smiles down at me. The cups and plates shift and she squeezes them and says, "There." Then she says, "Would you like to come aboard? We're practically back to normal here. We lost some books and charts, but Mr. Jura ran these enormous fans for hours and everything else has dried out quite well. I have coffee on in the cabin. You can have a cup and we can discuss your failed television career."

I look up at her and think about it.

"Or I could join *you!*" she says then. "Oh, that would be wonderful! You must understand, I've been utterly deserted, I have nothing whatever to do with myself, I've shopped myself silly already and can't afford any more of that, and I'd love to see just what it is you do out there." She stops and smiles. "Is it awfully rude to just invite myself along?"

"Maybe a little," I say, for some reason.

Mallory smiles like *she* knows why I said it. Then she gives a dramatic shrug—still hanging onto the plates and cups—and says, "Well, have a wonderful day, then. Try not to think of me dying of boredom while you're off swashbuckling on the high seas." She turns on her toes and takes a couple of steps and goes down into the wheel pit toward the cabin.

"Hold on," I say.

Mallory stops and looks back at me.

"We could go out for a little while," I say.

She smiles and drops the party debris into a waste can by the cabin door. Then she glides back to the stern. I move the skiff close and she steps onto the chrome ladder. I grab hold of the bottom rung and watch her climb down.

TWENTY-FIVE

Ducking forward as I row brings my head to within a few inches of Mallory's. She's facing me on the stern thwart with her knees aimed a little to the right and her hands tucked under her legs. "I like your boat!" she says as we pull up close.

"Thanks," I say.

"Who's Julie Marie?"

"My ex-wife."

"I'm *sorry*," she says.

"Yeah, me too."

I hold the skiff against the bigger boat while she climbs nimbly up and over. Then I pull myself along the hull, switch the lines, and roll up onto the foredeck. I step back and drop down behind the wheel. Mallory's standing aft, looking like a movie star in aviator sunglasses. I start the motor and head out past the island. I circle the ledge and swing in close to shore, where it's all woods and you can't see any of the town except for the church steeple. The trees are getting greener all the time, hiding things.

"I'm so happy you let me come along," Mallory says from just outside the wheelhouse.

"No problem," I say.

"Look!" She points toward the shore, at a dark, doggy head in the water. The seal looks back at us, then casually rolls under, shiny and bulky.

"Good-size boy," I say.

"Are there a lot of seals?"

"Oh yeah. You have to chase them out of the skiffs sometimes."

"Not really?"

"They like to sneak in and sun themselves. But they stink up the skiffs and tip them over when they climb out. Some of the guys used to shoot them on sight, but if they catch you now they'll fine you pretty heavy."

We come opposite a half dozen young shags standing with their wings out on the rocks. Mallory walks aft to watch them as we ride past. "What are they doing?" she calls back.

"Drying their wings. No oil in their feathers."

"How funny." She returns to her spot by the wheelhouse.

"I take it you haven't been a sailor for long?"

"Not long at all," she says.

"Where'd you grow up?"

"Ohio." She says it as if she's amazed.

I hold the boat in close to the shore. There are no houses along here, just water, rocks, and trees. Black ledges worn smooth, bleached gray above the high tide line. Driftwood here and there, and wild roses growing down over the rocks to the edge of the water.

"Lovely!" Mallory says. "Oh, smell them!"

"Sometimes you can smell them a mile out."

"Really?"

The water shallows and I turn us away from the shore. We scoot out into the bay toward Owls Head. Mallory goes aft again to stand in the wind with her chin in the air. The sun is well up over the islands now, but it's still cool in the breeze and she comes back into the wheelhouse before long. I look at her and she smiles. She's got her hands in her back pockets, which makes her breasts hang against the front of her jersey, and for some reason the fact that they're not on the same stripe lets me picture them, plump and goosebumped.

"Where are we going?" Mallory asks.

I nod out toward Big Branch.

"Is that where your traps are?"

"Out that way."

The *Julie Marie* is running smooth and clean. To starboard the Rockland Breakwater stretches in a perfectly straight line halfway into the harbor. To port are the humpbacked, blue-colored Havens and Big Branch.

Mallory doesn't say anything for a time, and I don't either: I'm a little short of breath with her and her breasts so close. We steam out into deep water, opposite Owls Head Light and then, after a while, the Number Two Point, jutting up high and rocky, like a miniature Rock of Gibraltar.

"Tell me the best thing you've ever seen," Mallory says then.

"I don't know," I say. "You see dolphins. They're pretty cool." I don't much like the question. I'm afraid I'll start boring her, like I did at the Lord Pequot.

"What else?" she says.

"Oh, fish hawks," I say. "You know, ospreys. You see them hanging into the breeze, like they're on a wire. An eagle once in a while. A bald. Once in a great while a golden. You see herons pretty often."

"I love herons. They're so prehistoric!"

I turn the boat a bit southerly.

"What about whales?"

"Once in a while," I say.

"We saw one sailing up. They're so huge!"

"Their *tails* are bigger than anything else in the water," I say.

"I wish we'd see one."

"Maybe we will."

"I'd die," she says.

But we don't see any whales. The bay stays wide and flat, the water shivering in different-size patches here and there. After a while I ask if she minds if I smoke. I'm still nervous, wondering how I'm coming across. I don't *want* to care, but I can't help it.

"You're the captain," she says.

"Want one?"

"I'm really not supposed to smoke," she says.

"Okay."

"No, I'd love one," she says, and laughs.

I shake a couple out of the pack, strike the match, shield it with my hands. I flip the match overboard. She nips the smoke in, blows a stream out that hooks toward the stern.

I turn the *Julie Marie* toward the southern tip of Big Branch.

"You wouldn't have anything to drink, would you?" Mallory says.

I look at her.

"Joke," she smiles.

We ride out steadily toward Big Branch. It's warmer, but looking at Mallory, it's obvious she's still cold. Clam heads, Polky calls them. As in: "Check out the clam heads!" Mallory is looking to her left, and I'm checking them out, all right. Then she puts her hands behind her head and stretches, which draws the jersey taut. Somehow that puts them onto the same stripe, and I drool down the wrong pipe and start coughing.

"Are you all right?" Mallory says.

I cough and clear my throat and cough again until it hurts my lungs. She thumps me on the back, and after a while it's better. My eyes are watering, though. I wipe them on my sleeve, look at Mallory, and we both laugh.

We run the rest of the way to my first set of traps, and I slow and turn toward the buoys slanting in the water. I lean out with the gaff and yank the line up onto the snatch block. Then I pull it in and take a turn around the hauler. Mallory's standing close, and when the trap comes swelling to the surface I say, "Watch out."

She steps back. I snap the line free and pull the trap splashing up onto the rail. I open the trap and pick out the starfish and sea urchins and throw them overboard. There are little lobsters that I throw over, too. Likewise a berried female, whose tail I notch before I toss her back. Then a couple of keepers, one close enough to measure. I band their claws and drop them into the well. I don't have any bait along—just as well, with Mallory aboard—so I leave the old bait bag in the trap, slide it off the rail, and head for the next buoy while the trap falls off into the water.

"You're so efficient!" Mallory says.

We chug along from set to set, and manage to take four keepers over the next hour. "That'll give you something for lunch," I say.

"Really?" she says. "Oh, I couldn't."

"Fresh off the boat," I say.

We start off again, and I guide her away from the line that's drooped onto the deck and is whipping after the trap over the side. It probably wouldn't do to lose her overboard. She puts her hands on my arm, and for a second or two we stand still that way. Then the line is all gone and she lets go. We step over to the well, where the four lobsters are marching around in slow-motion.

"That'll do it," I say. "We can head back."

"May I have another cigarette?"

I hand her one.

"It's really too bad we don't have a bottle of wine," she says. "And some sandwiches. We could have a picnic on a beach! There are so many little islands! Don't you think it would be fun?"

"Sure."

I swing us around. We drop Big Branch behind and cruise in toward the mainland. Pretty soon the seagulls show up and flock behind us, making their greedy noises. They trail us back past Number Two Point and Bobby Lawson's beach and Owls Head Light sitting on its high point. I look past the Rockland Breakwater and see a Coast Guard cutter—white with the orange blaze down its side—tied up at the Coast Guard dock.

Mallory tosses her cigarette overboard, crosses her arms, and moves closer to the stack.

"Cold?"

"A little."

"I have a sweatshirt below," I say, "but I don't know if it's anything you'd want to wear."

Mallory tips her head, looks at me. "I have a better idea," she says.

I feel my face go hot, but I turn toward her, keeping one hand on the wheel, lifting the other so she can put her arms around my waist. She tucks her face in close and squeezes her body against mine. I touch her forehead with my lips and notice how much taller than Niki she is.

"*Much* better," Mallory says. She locks her hands together behind me. Tall and slender, she's a lot to hold. I feel her all around me and my hips sort of twitch against her. She wiggles back. It seems plenty warm in the cockpit now. I correct our course a fraction and we ride on toward Pequot without speaking. At first you can't see any breaks in the shoreline, but as I steer toward the steeple the harbor begins to open up around it.

Mallory says, "Troy Hull?" into my neck.

I clear my throat. "Uh-huh?"

"When we get back, I'll invite you aboard again. Would that be all right?"

"Okay," I manage to say.

She tips her head back, lifts her sunglasses to the top of her head, and looks at me. "I could show you the cabin," she says. "Maybe we could have a drink *there*." She smiles dreamily.

"Sure," I say.

"And then," she says, "do you think you could just fuck me and get it over with?" She ducks her face back into my neck and shivers against me. I feel the blush start at my toes and move all the way up through my body.

TWENTY-SIX

We run along toward Pequot, holding onto each other. My face is hot and I have to clear my throat. I'm pretty damn flummoxed. Mallory leans back and looks at me again. Now she's got the same bright, trembly look she had at the landing when we kissed. Her whole body seems to be vibrating. We kiss and she puts her hands on my chest and lets her head hang back. Her sunglasses fall behind her to the deck. I reach out and throttle the engine back.

"We don't *have* to wait," she whispers, and that's when I feel the first goddamn hesitation. I try to ignore it, I kiss her again, but then she slides her hands between us and this little panic stirs inside me and I can't seem to do anything about it. My damn ears start ringing. It's all happening too fast. I thought we'd have the ride back, but she's acting like she wants it right now. The thoughts take me over then, and pretty soon I know it's a lost cause, and I just hold myself still and wait.

After a second or two her eyes blink open.

"Is something wrong?" she says, and I can see her coming back, still breathing fast and shallow, but her eyes are losing the brightness. When I don't say anything she clears her throat and laughs under her breath. She stands up on her toes and kisses my nose. "Are we a little shy?" she says. Then she says, "My goodness!" and brushes the damp hair off her forehead.

I hold her, feeling stupid. The boat wallows and we sway together to keep our balance.

"I didn't think *anyone* was shy any more!" she says. "Do you think I'm an awful woman to be so terribly forward?"

I try to laugh.

"Poor baby." Mallory hugs me close. "I'm sorry."

I push the throttle in and start us toward Pequot again, but I don't let go of Mallory, I don't want her to stand apart from me. My ears are still ringing, and the goddamn blood's run out of me, but if she moves away it'll all come to an end. I give the *Julie Marie* a little more gas and the engine rises into a steady watery growl.

"*I'm* sorry," I say.

"Don't be," she says. "This is perfectly nice, all by itself."

I look at the shoreline, watch it shift and grow.

"We'll just snuggle," Mallory says. "I'm sorry I was so crass."

"It's not your fault."

"Yes it is. I ruined it, didn't I?"

"You didn't ruin anything."

"Oh, yes I did. I could tell."

"Could you stop talking, please?" I say. The blood's rising in me again and I don't want to chatter it away. I'm getting brave again. But not brave enough to pick up where we left off. I still want the trip in. If I take a while to settle down then, well, okay, I'm shy.

We close on Pequot harbor, and when we pass the island Mallory stands off to the side. That leaves me embarrassed at the way I'm configured. But I'm relieved, too. My damn *shyness* has pulled back into a little corner, and I can see us lying together, taking our time. I'm feeling a little urgent, even. Then I notice Reese's dinghy tied up astern of the sailboat. So that takes care of that.

We ride alongside Danny's pier, seaweed waving in our wash.

Mallory says, "I suppose you'd better let me off at Danny's."

"If you think," I say.

"Even though you were a perfect gentleman," she says.

"I'm sorry," I say again.

She laughs softly.

I swing over to the pier and back off the engine. We drift up to the third float where the gangway angles down. The tide's pretty low.

I pull the *Julie Marie* in snug, and Mallory puts her arms around my waist and holds me close. "No, Troy Hull," she says. "*I'm* sorry." She's got the old amused smile on her face.

"You shouldn't be."

"You don't think I'm a terrible woman?"

"Of course not."

"Oh, God," she says, and laughs. "All right, I'm going now." She pecks me on the lips, walks out of the wheelhouse, steps up on the rail and down to the float.

I follow. "What about your lobsters?"

"I really couldn't." She shrugs without taking her fingers out of her pockets, smiles, and sets off up the gangway. I watch her go, *yearning* after her like a bloody eighth-grader. She reaches the pier and disappears. I stand there with my hands on my hips, trying to keep my spirits from sinking *too* far. I tell myself I don't want to get mixed up with someone like her anyway.

"Yeah, right," I say.

I snap the line free, coil it, and tuck it against the rail. Then I fire up the engine, steer over to my mooring, tie up the boat, bucket the lobsters, climb down into the skiff. I strike a match and light a smoke, letting myself drift off from the *Julie*. I'm working the oars into the locks, trying to keep the smoke out of my eyes, when I hear someone clear his throat, and I look over my shoulder to see Charles Reese standing at the stern of the *Bluefin*.

I swing the skiff around and the *Bluefin* comes into view again. Reese is still standing there, hands on his hips and his hair blowing around.

"You got a problem?" I say.

He doesn't answer, just looks toward Danny's, like he knows that's where Mallory went, then turns and heads back into the cabin and shuts the door.

I sit in the skiff, the water restless around me. I'm ready to head in, but there's still that business with Danny. I could go and see him as planned. But I'm more inclined to just go home. I feel more like punching myself than punching Danny. I think it over for a minute or two, then dig the oars into the water and head for the bridge.

TWENTY-SEVEN

The next couple days don't go any better. The haul sucks so bad on Wednesday I don't even make enough to pay for bait and gas. And then, coming home from the pound, I see Polky steaming out and think I'll at least be able to get a few things off my chest, but he veers away and heads out toward the Havens, like he's avoiding me—like *I'm* the one who's been pestering *him*.

I mean, Jesus. But that's not the half of it.

Later that same afternoon, I walk downtown to buy the newspaper and spot Mallory coming out of Maine-ly Drugs. I get all buoyed up to see her, and I cross the street. She wheels along with her head down, looking at the headlines on her newspaper, and I wait on the sidewalk in front of the grocery store. When she gets close I say, "Hey, Mallory!"

She looks up, gives me a fake smile, says, "Hello, Troy Hull," and breezes right on by. I watch her walk away, watch her cross to the green, and then I go into the drugstore, buy the paper, and take it home.

I'm feeling like quite a guy.

Thursday comes along and the catch is even worse. When I check my numbers at Cormier's, it's shaping up to be my worst week ever. Seeing it in black and white is shocking. I'm hardly able to muster a hello and goodbye to Stan.

Back at the creek I take a long snooze, but nothing looks any different when I wake up, aside from it being dark out. Nor does it later, down at Captain Cobb's, even after three beers. I'm wondering what the hell I ever did except try to be a half-decent husband and have a few now and then and work hard and try to make a living. I never cheated on my wife, nor even wanted to, so why the hell should I have to worry about that side of things?

Molly Ring comes over with another beer. "Tell me what happened," she says, real low. It's the first chance we've had to talk since the other night.

I sip my beer, put it down. "Well, the clam cops showed up."

"Oh, no," Molly says.

"Did you do like I asked?"

"Uh-huh," she says. "He asked what you were up to, and I said, 'That's a good question.' Then we talked it over a little and I made believe I was worried about you. I said I thought you had some deal going tonight."

"What'd he do then?"

"Finished his beer and took off."

"Took off to make a call," I say.

She shakes her head sadly, then walks down to the taps to pour Rankin a beer. He nods to me, and I nod back. Molly comes over and says, "Why would he do that, Troy?"

"I think they might have him over a barrel."

She leans back with both elbows on the counter. "Sometimes I just don't know," she says.

"Tell me about it."

A gang of young *professionals* barges into the place then, grabbing all the free seats at the bar, and forcing Molly back into her cheerful work mode. I take ten minutes to finish my burger and beer and then I get up and say goodnight.

"Be good," Molly says from the taps.

Outside I stand on the sidewalk. It's a little cool out and there's some traffic, a few people walking around. I'm not sure what to do with myself, but there seems to be more resistance toward home, so I go the other way, crossing the river and, on impulse, taking a right into the marine park. I haven't been here for a while. It's hilly with paved footpaths and granite curbs, and imported shrubs and wrought-iron benches under lights made to look like old-time lanterns.

I head straight through, passing another guy walking with his head down. The lane comes out to Harbor Street, which I follow past several blocks of old sea captains' homes and maple trees to the end of the point and Danny's marina. I guess this is where I was headed all along.

I stand under a maple in the dark, then skulk across the muddy yard full of forklifts, tugs, golf carts, and boat trailers. At one end are the tarped boats, up on stanchions, waiting to go back in the water. I pass the big-wheeled lift that stands in front of the boat launch, and walk out onto the pier that runs along the waterfront. There's a spotlight at one end, but the other is dark so I walk down there and sit in the shadow of the hoist. It's cooler on the water, and I pull my jacket around me. The salt water lifts and slaps against granite footings.

The *Bluefin* is only a hundred feet away. She's moving lightly, turnbuckles clanging against her metal mast. The rubber dinghy is tied astern, there's light in the cabin, and I can hear voices. I picture Mallory sitting with perfect posture on a bunk, drinking a glass of wine, and I think about the way she walked past me on the street. It hurts. I never thought I'd get my hands on someone like her, and then I blew my chance, so now, instead of remembering how sweet it was, I have to sit here and feel like a goddamn idiot.

I light a cigarette, smoke it cupped in my hand. I light another off that one and pitch the butt into the water. The air gets cooler. I don't know what I'm waiting for, but can't get myself to leave. Then I hear Reese's voice, louder than before. When he stops there's no answer from Mallory, but then the cabin door opens and she comes out. She shuts the door with a little bang, and I guess maybe that's her answer. I hunch deeper into the shadows, drop the butt into the water. With my jeans and dark hoodie, I'm pretty well concealed. I remember when we were kids we wore dark clothes and put dirt on our faces when we snuck around, and if we sat perfectly still no one ever saw us.

Mallory takes the cockpit steps and stands at the stern, hugging herself with one arm, sipping from a drink in her other hand, and swaying a little with the boat. She's wearing jeans and a light sweater, and her hair is pulled back behind her ears with a dark headband holding it in place. She looks so good I almost call out to her. But even *I'm* not that stupid. A few seconds later the cabin door opens again, and Charles Reese comes out and looks at her, with his hands moving around in his pockets.

"Mallory?" he says.

She doesn't even look back.

"I'm sorry I raised my voice," he says.

Mallory takes a sip of her drink.

"I was reacting on a primitive level. I realize that now."

It's momentarily quiet; I listen to the turnbuckles.

"Did you forget whose idea it was in the first place?" she says then, very evenly.

"I haven't forgotten." Reese climbs out of the cockpit and walks over, but she just stares out at the bay. "I really thought it would add a little spice to our lives," he says. "I thought we could get away with it up here. But I suppose I was picturing some advertising type. Someone like that fellow who flirted with you at the Christmas party, remember? We had some fun with that, and it made me think that we could be a little more . . . I don't know . . . daring? But never in my wildest dreams did I imagine you'd run off with one of the local yokels."

"Really?" Mallory says.

"It was a shock."

"It was still your idea," she says.

"It was a wretched idea."

They go quiet again, and I listen to the turnbuckles and the creak of the shifting floats and the slap of the water. Cool air brushes past my face. I think the breeze might be picking up.

"I *am* sorry, Mal," Reese says. "It was wrong of me." He slips an arm around her waist. "Please?" he says.

Mallory looks at her drink, rattles the ice.

"Pretty please?" Reese says.

She laughs softly. Then she tips her head sideways, rests it on Reese's shoulder.

"It was just an experiment that didn't pan out," Reese says.

"It certainly was that."

"It means nothing in the grand scheme of things."

"Good."

"As long as you won't be going native again any time soon."

"I hardly think so," Mallory says.

Reese turns and hugs her. She puts one arm around his neck, holds the drink out to the side. They press tightly together and kiss. Then they stand with their arms around each other, looking out at the water. After a while Reese whispers something, and they wander back down the steps into the cockpit. Reese opens the cabin door, and when she turns and steps down, he clears his throat and says, "I suppose it *was* a walk on the wild side, eh?"

She looks out the doorway at him.

"If nothing else," Reese says. His voice has gotten a little husky.

Mallory laughs and says, "God, we deserve each other." She backs down the cabin steps and Reese follows, pulling the door quickly shut behind him.

When the cabin goes dark I get up, stiff and chilled. I slop through the yard, walk down the street, and turn into the park. Back on Main Street I re-cross the river, looking between buildings at the water, passing the shops with their nightlights and *Closed* signs and their awnings cranked in close. At the square I turn up Seaview, pass the movie theater and the steak house, Erky's wharf and the single-story block of stores. Near the top of the hill a car passes and goes on across the bridge: *whump, whump.*

Halfway down Hull I hear the airy sound of a bouncing basketball, and when I get to my driveway there's Polky, standing under the hoop, catching the ball as it falls through, dribbling it twice and spinning it up off the backboard underhanded.

I see his Harley parked out of the way, off to the side.

I'm in no great mood for company, but Polky hears me on the crushed rock and turns to snap a two-handed pass my way. I catch it and fire it right back—that's just hoop protocol. Polky snags the ball, fakes one way, turns, and flips it up off the backboard. "Two!" he says. "At the buzzer!" He one-hands the ball behind his back to me, and I drain a little jumper. He grabs the ball on one bounce and whips it back to me. I walk over, open the pickup's door, and toss it behind the seat.

He leads the way to the deck and up the steps. He's strutting more than usual, as if good things have been happening. It makes me feel worse by comparison. A beer bottle sits on the table, and he grabs it and tips his head back to take a slug. I circle the little table and sit down.

"Well?" Polky says with a big grin. He's looming over me, holding the beer bottle down by his hip.

"Well, what?" I say.

"Well, did you see me on TV?"

"No, but I heard about it."

"Jesus, you missed it? I was a mother-fucking TV star!"

"Did you really call him *Chummy?*"

"Damn right I did! But I was a good boy, mostly. I was like, 'We all have to work together to preserve our way of life!'" He points the bottle at me, careful not to spill any. "Now *you*," he says, "would've shot your mouth off, because you ain't too bright."

"Thank you," I say.

"No problem." He raises the bottle. "Couple more where this came from."

"Maybe later."

He sits down at the table and looks at me proudly, like he's got more good stuff to tell. But then he squints, like he's trying to read my mind. Finally he says, "All right, what's going on?"

"I don't even know where to begin," I say.

"Start anywhere, it don't matter."

I think it over for about three seconds, and then go ahead and tell him about Danny, the ride out to Big Branch, and the clam cops showing up right on schedule.

His eyes get narrow. "That little fucker. I knew it!"

"Yup."

Polky drums his fingers. Then he puts his hands flat on the table. "All right, that does it," he says. "We need to talk business. I got this thing all worked out to a T, and there's no fucking reason why you should let them box you into a corner when you could jump on board instead."

I just look at him, feeling wicked tired.

He stares back, and I wait for him to get grumpy, because I'm *still* not telling him what he wants to hear. But he doesn't, for some reason. He goes the other way, in fact. His face relaxes, he crosses his arms on his chest, and leans back in his chair, like he's confident all he has to do is give me a few seconds. It turns out that he's right. It works just like he's expecting. Something flies into me from out of the dark. Something *reckless* flies up and dives into my gut and roils the anger and frustration.

Polky grins, like it shows on my face.

"Okay," I say. "Spill it."

He hunches the chair up close, holds his claw out flat over the table. "Picture one of them little Cessnas," he says, "way out by The Havens, maybe." He swoops his hand down and says, "There's a splash,"—he banks his hand away—"then off it goes. And I'm Johnny-on-the-spot, see? But not you, Troy-boy, you don't even come into it yet. You're still on shore. You're getting ready to meet me at the old fire station and follow me out 17 to that garage where we used to get our stickers."

"Kimball's old place?"

"Right. When I turn in there," Polky says, "you go on past and hang a left up the hill. Cut your lights and pull in behind that old barn beside the road. Sit back and enjoy the show. There's a woods road from the top of the hill that goes down behind the garage, and if anything funny happens, throw your lights on and come charging to the rescue. That's it. You're backup, that's all."

"Sounds kind of serious," I say.

"Oh, we're not fucking around. But here's the thing: it's a one-time deal. I've been thinking about what you said, believe it or not—especially with Moody and his little sidekick sniffing around. I figure a lot of little deals just gives them more cracks at you. So instead, we make one big score, you pay a big chunk of what you owe off to the dump-bird, so they can't grab your house, and I take care of a couple of things, and we give it a year or so for the fishing to turn around."

"You can make that much in one deal?" I say.

"*This* deal you can."

We sit there looking at each other. He's trimmed his beard down and, with his hair pulled back into the ponytail, he looks almost clean cut. I figure they made him do it for his TV appearance.

"All we're doing," he says, "is transferring something from somebody I know to somebody I don't know. It's the one I don't know that has me a little *cautious*. Just because I don't know them," he says, "not because I'm *expecting* any trouble."

"What kind of something?" I say.

He just sits there with his innocent face on.

"Be right back," I say. In the kitchen I stand by the fridge, thinking it over. But it's like steaming someplace in a thick fog. Everything shifts and changes shape and you can't make any sense of it. Eventually you just make a move. The reckless feeling comes over me again, and I go onto the deck and hand Polky a beer. He twists the cap off and holds the bottle out over the table. I sit down and tap mine carefully against his.

He drains his beer in big swallows, puts the empty down. "Okay," he says. "Saturday night, midnight, the old fire station. I'll let you know if anything changes."

"This Saturday?"

"No, dumbass, *last* Saturday!" He claps me on the shoulder and heads down the steps, giving me the finger as he walks around the deck. He kick-starts the Harley, spins it on the crushed rock as he leaves. He sputters to the corner, revs down the hill. Then it's quiet. I stand up and look out at my yard and think about what I've just done.

Looking into the darkness, I wonder what's moving around. Sometimes deer cross to get to the creek. I've seen their footprints. And other critters, too: foxes, beavers, coyotes. Out in the river seals, otters, ducks, loons, geese, shags, fish hawks, eagles. I saw a gyrfalcon once, pure white like a seagull, but a quick, serious flyer.

I think about Donald Hartley in a brand new house, with the land all posted. Then I walk down off the deck and across the lawn, and sidestep down the bank to the edge of the creek. There's a big flat rock down there you can stand on when the water's low. I step over to the rock and listen to the water rushing toward the bridge. I crouch like a catcher with one hand on the rock to keep my balance, and feel the fine spray on my face.

TWENTY-EIGHT

The next morning I start out just before sunrise, rowing down the creek through the sea smoke. I ride under the bridge and across the harbor to the *Julie Marie*, barely glancing at the dark shape of the *Bluefin*, and thinking: To hell with those swanks. I put out past the island with the throttle a touch above idle, the water all silvery, the horizon beginning to lighten eastward. I look around at the bay and the shore and the dark humpbacked islands and I sip from my thermos cup. I listen to the weatherman on the radio, and when he's finished I throttle up and head for the grounds. I start in hauling and lo and behold, the goddamn traps are coming up rich. I can almost hear the gods laughing. It stays like that all day, and when I get back to the pound, a couple of other guys are fired up over their hauls, too.

Heading home with my bill half paid and money in my pocket, I wonder about the deal with Polky. If you hit a real hot streak, you can make a lot of money fast. But the more I think it through, the more I realize that it won't make any difference. There's no way they're going to leave me alone. Hartley and Keith Zeiglaar and Trace White and the clam cops and even Danny Brinker are going to make sure that it won't be enough. I'm going to have to stick with Polky and hope *that* doesn't turn out bad. Because if it does, I'll not only lose my house, I'll lose the *Julie Marie*, too. She'll probably become another Marine Patrol boat under command of Dickless Tracy Thibeault.

So there it is.

I run the rest of the way in past the island in the strong afternoon light, resigned again, and in a pretty good mood because of it.

What the hell, I think, we'll just see what happens. When you don't have any choices, there's no sense worrying.

I cut the engine and drift with the gaff in my hand, but before I reach the mooring I hear the *Bluefin*'s cabin door shut and look over to see Mallory come out of the cockpit, wearing white pants that stop just below her knees and the same striped jersey she wore on our boat ride. Her hair is wet and pulled into a ponytail, and she's saying something over her shoulder to Charles Reese, who's coming out right behind her.

I start my engine back up and turn away from the mooring. Mallory looks over at the sound, raising a hand to shade her eyes. Reese comes up beside her. When Mallory waves, I raise a hand an inch or two.

"Hello, Troy Hull!" she calls out.

I raise my hand again and head toward the landing. I don't look back at them until I'm near the float. Then I see Reese steering Mallory toward the cabin, his arm around her, her arms pinned against her sides and her head down.

On the near float, Freddie Linscott is hosing down his launch, his pinned-up sleeve flapping every time he moves. He turns to watch me bring the *Julie Marie* in.

"I got a little chain problem out there," I explain to him.

"Sure then, no problem," Freddie says.

"Thanks, man."

"How you doing, anyway?" Freddie holds the hose out to the side, lets it splash onto the aluminum walkway connecting his float to the one the TV people have been using.

"Oh, I'm brand new," I say.

He grins and flips the stream in a little salute. Then he goes back to work, looking up at me when I pass him on the walkway. I cross over to the TV float and go up the gangway to the boardwalk. I hoof it up to the five-way, look in Cobb's window, and see Polky sitting at the bar. I'd go in and join him, but I need to shower and change first. I turn around to walk past the movie theater and the steakhouse. The steakhouse is busy: you can see the suits leaning on the bar and sitting at the window tables. I wonder if Danny and his new friends are in there, making plans.

That's all right, I've got my own plans.

We'll just see whose plans work out best.

I pass Erky's wharf and the tourist traps. A middle-aged couple steps out of a shop that sells brass goods, and when they give me the old look, I say, "Don't let it bother you." They squeeze over and walk past without saying anything.

TWENTY-NINE

Polky's still hunched at the bar in his denim jacket, taking up enough room for two normal-size guys. His ponytail is hanging down between his shoulder blades, and his feet are on the brass rail, his jeans rolled halfway up on his boots.

Molly finishes refilling the straw and napkin holder and bends down to lift a rack of glasses off the floor. She grabs a glass in each hand, slides them stem-first into the overhead rack, and dives into the rack for two more. She smiles and says, "Hey, sweetie."

"Hey, Molly."

Polky turns and grins at me. I swing myself up onto a stool. I stretch, my hands touching the netting overhead.

Molly heads off with the empty glasses rack.

Polky looks at my wet hair and says, "You go out today?"

"Yup."

"How was it?"

"Not bad for a change."

Molly comes back from the kitchen with another rack of glasses. She's turned the collar up on her Cobb's jersey. The kitchen door swings shut behind her and she heaves the rack up onto the bar.

"Molly," Polky says. "Buy my friend here a pint."

"You don't have any friends." Molly makes stacks of rocks glasses and sets them on the bar.

"And a couple of schnapps, since you're not busy."

"Hold your horses," Molly says.

Polky looks at me. "You come in here to spend some of your goddamn hard-earned money?"

Molly laughs and swings the empty rack under the bar. She pours us beers, slides two shot glasses over and tops them with peppermint schnapps. Then she leans against the liquor cabinet with her arms crossed, looking at us with a little smile on her lips.

"Mud in your eye," Polky says.

We down our shots and chase them with beer. Polky pushes his shot glass toward Molly. It leaves a wet trail across the shiny wood.

"Are we having ourselves an evening?" Molly says.

"Could be," Polky says.

"Anybody driving?"

"I walked down," I say, and push my shot glass up beside Polky's.

"I'll stay at Troy's," Polky says.

"Promise?"

He puts his hand on the dog-eared Mr. Boston next to the napkin holder. "I swear on the bible!" he says. Then he takes a twenty out of his pocket and stuffs it into Molly's tip jar. Molly hips herself away from the cabinet and grabs the schnapps bottle off the shelf.

We drink and whisper about Saturday night. When I ask him again what we'll be transferring, he says, "Listen, it don't matter. One delivery more or less ain't going to make any big difference no matter what it is. Except it'll make a big difference for *us*. And if I get out of it afterward it'll make a difference that way too, won't it? Your tender little heart can think about that!" He catches Molly's eye and points two fingers down at our shot glasses, but I put my hand over mine.

"Never mind," Polky says. "I guess we're on hold."

"Good idea," Molly says.

I sip my beer, lick foam off my lips. It's pretty quiet in the place. There was a rush earlier, but it was mostly locals who've gone home, and the place has mellowed again. The paper-pushers haven't shown up at all. I figure they're still at the steakhouse. I enjoy their absence right up until Niki Harjula walks in with two of them in tow, and then I get a little offended. I turn around for a better look at their *swank* mannerisms: tug the trousers when you sit, pull the cuffs into place, tuck the hair behind the ears, check the Rolex.

Niki's still dressed for work. I can tell she knows I'm here by the way she doesn't look at me.

I turn back around.

Molly sails over to take their order, lifting the trap at the end of the bar. She comes back and I watch her take down the Courvoisier bottle, and then I look at Niki again, in the mirror. It bugs me that she's with these suits, but I remember that I had *my* chance and didn't do anything with it. Back before I also didn't do anything with Mallory Reese.

Niki meets my eyes in the mirror, stands up from the booth, comes up to the bar, and sits next to me. "Hi, Troy," she says.

"Hi Niki," I say.

Polky looks past me. "Niki Harjula!"

"Hi, Billy. I like the new look."

"You do?"

"Yeah, you look like Alec Baldwin."

"No shit?" Polky tips his head, checks himself in the mirror.

Niki smiles at me.

Polky says, "You kids excuse me," and lumbers off to the men's room at the far end of the joint. I don't know if he's just giving us a moment—Polky has manners once in a while—or whether he wants to see if he really does look like Baldwin. He goes in and shuts the door.

Niki twines her hands on the bar and looks up at me. For a second it's almost like a swank woman is sitting there, with her modern hair and her nice clothes. Then she speaks and it's definitely Niki again. "I just wanted to say I'm sorry about the other night, Troy," she says. It comes out like she rehearsed it.

"Don't be silly," I say.

"No, I get stupid sometimes."

"It wasn't you, anyway," I say. "It was me."

"What do you mean?"

"I didn't know what to say."

"About what?"

"I'll explain it sometime."

Niki puts a hand on my arm. "Explain it now."

"Naw, I need to think about how to do it."

One of Niki's friends calls, and she turns and says, "Just a second!" Then she swings back, like she has more to say to me. But Polky slams the bathroom door and heads back our way, and Niki sighs and gets down off the stool. "I could stop in tonight and we could talk," she says.

"Okay, but I think Polky's staying over."

She looks at Polky lumbering toward us. "I guess I'll wait, then," she says. She leans against me, kisses my cheek, and goes back to the booth.

Polky sits down. "We ready for a couple more?"

"Why not?" I say.

"Molly!" Polky fumbles in his pocket and stuffs another twenty into the tip jar. Molly rolls her eyes, but reaches for the schnapps bottle. We down the shots and sip beer, and Polky waves for a refill. I watch Niki and her pals in the mirror as they finish their drinks and slide out of the booth.

"Why's she hanging with that crowd?" Polky says. He's watching, too, as the swanky boys head with Niki to the door. She's short enough to make them look tall.

"Who knows?" I say.

"She used to be a nice girl."

"She's still nice," I say.

Niki's group leaves and the door shuts.

"You shoulda snagged that a long time ago," Polky says, nudging me.

"I was married."

"You ain't married now."

"Well, neither are you," I say.

He looks seriously at me. "I don't want a nice girl," he says. Then his eyes get wide and he breaks out giggling. I grin back and that pretty much sets the tone as the evening goes forward. Everything gets real funny. I laugh until my cheeks hurt at Polky's comments, Molly's winks. On the TV a sitcom about a woman and her landlord seems hilarious, even though I can't make out much of what they're saying. Everything's a big gag. It's so funny that when the Reeses come waltzing in an hour or so later, I even laugh at that.

THIRTY

The Reeses take the same booth Niki and her friends were in. I think it's pretty amazing that they've shown up. It's like I'm in some dumb movie, and this is part of the script. I've got Alec Baldwin sitting beside me. Now Mallory is across the room, who might as well be a movie star. And who would play Reese? Dan Akroyd, maybe? What about Molly? I look closely at her, but no one comes to mind right away.

What about you? I think then.

But my face in the mirror doesn't look like any movie star. Lassie, maybe, with the long nose and shaggy hair.

"Drink up, Viking boy," Alec Baldwin says.

I laugh, and it comes out like a bark.

Molly squints at me.

I say, "Sorry."

She shakes her head.

In the mirror I see Reese hold two fingers up, and Molly turns to splash Grand Marnier into snifters. She takes them to the booth, and when she comes back I say, "What, they've got a standing order?"

Molly shrugs.

"Fucking TV people," Polky says.

"Look who's talking," I say.

"Viking boy!"

"TV boy!"

"*What* are you two idiots yapping about?" Molly says.

Polky laughs like he's helpless. Every time he looks at me I lose it, too. This goes on for a while. Finally I get myself under control and focus on the booth again. I watch my favorite swanks. After a little I realize everything might not be hunky-dory over there. Reese is smirking at Mallory, but she won't look back at him. He leans forward like he's trying to get low enough to see into her downcast eyes, and when she puts a hand to her brow he takes hold of her wrist and says something. She pulls her arm away and puts her hands in her lap. Reese gets out of the booth and says, "Come on, you should at least say hello. I mean, after *all!*"

Mallory looks down at her lap.

Reese takes her arm, puts his other hand behind her back, and sort of eases her to her feet. I'm guessing that he must be in the middle of another *primitive* reaction to our boat ride. When he walks Mallory toward us, I swing around on my stool, a little in awe of the situation.

Polky turns around too, and I say, "Let me deal with it."

"That's okay," Polky says.

I look back at the Reeses. Mallory has put her hand to her forehead. "Charles," she says, "can we just go?"

"Where are your manners?" Reese says.

Molly Ring says, "Is everything all right?"

"Just lovely!" Reese says. He walks Mallory closer, holding her as if she might stumble, stopping a pace away. "We couldn't help overhearing all the hilarity," he says. "Why don't you ask them just what is so funny, darling? As if we can't guess!"

"Charles, enough is enough."

Reese looks at Polky. "Listen," he says, "you just happened to be handy. Right time and place. Your lucky day. So don't think you're anything special, okay?"

"Don't you mean me?" I say.

"I'm talking to the Incredible Hulk, there."

I look at Polky. He's staring at Reese.

"Tell him," Reese says to Mallory. He takes her in his arms then and kisses her. She jerks her head away, but he only laughs and kisses her again, bending her backwards. That's when Polky jumps off the stool, smacking a hand down on Reese's mop of hair and yanking him away from Mallory. Mallory nearly falls, but I grab her. She pushes my hands away, steps back, keeps her eyes on her husband and Polky.

Polky has a handful of Reese's shirt now, has pushed that fist up under his jaw and is walking him backwards, knocking a chair over, making the people at the table scramble out of his way.

"Billy!" Molly shouts.

"That's enough!" Reese croaks, pawing at Polky's hand.

But Polky's got that look. He shoves Reese higher on his toes, moving him toward the door, and when Reese tries to speak again he can't, because Polky's knuckles have twisted up against his windpipe. Reese's mouth is working, but no sound is coming out.

Molly comes around the end of the bar, a bus boy and the cook appear too, and the four of us circle them. Polky isn't paying us any mind. Reese is gagging and has both of his hands on Polky's wrist.

I move in and say, "Better let him go."

"You keep out of this," Polky growls.

Then Mallory rushes over and tries to yank Polky's arm away. She jerks and tugs like somebody trying to open a stuck door—with no effect whatsoever—and screeches, "Let him go!"

Polky stops and looks down at her. I must be still in movie-mode, because I picture King Kong looking at Jessica Lang while the choppers circle the World Trade Center.

Mallory is tugging away, wailing.

"He's *choking*," I tell Polky.

"Open the door, then," Polky says with disgust.

I open it, and Polky throws Reese outside. Reese staggers, coughing, hands at his throat, and Mallory slips through just before the door bangs shut. When Polky yanks the door open again, there's Mallory with her hands on Reese's arm, guiding him hacking toward the street corner.

Polky throws the door shut. "I will *never* understand swank women."

"That makes two of us," I say.

"What the hell did you think *you* were going to do?"

"Whatever," I say.

Molly says, "Thank you, Billy!" and heads for the bar. The bus boy and the cook go back to the kitchen, and the customers rearrange themselves at their table, making sure not to catch Polky's eye as he walks by. At the bar Polky gulps the rest of his beer, straddles the stool, shakes his head.

I sit beside him. "So what was that all about?"

"What the hell do you think?" Polky says.

"I don't know, that's why I'm asking."

He laughs, kind of bitter. Then he grins at me, looks over at Molly, and starts in. Pretty soon, everything begins to make a lot more sense. It turns out Polky took Mallory for a ride, too. He met her after his appearance on the TV show, and they talked for a while on the boardwalk, and at one point Mallory asked him if he ever took poor abandoned women for boat rides, and he said, "Oh yeah, that's practically all I do."

Molly laughs at that, and I pretend to.

Polky figured she was bullshitting, although you never knew with swank women, occasionally they got tired of their swank men. And then a couple of days later he was at the landing and she came walking up and off they went.

"The day you avoided me," I say.

"I was kinda busy, yeah!" he snickers.

It all sounds pretty familiar from that point, except that Polky didn't chicken out. He took her right down to his cuddy, on his smelly old V-bunk. He says she screeched like a hungry seagull and scratched the hell out of his back. "We pretty much went corner-to-corner," he says, as if he still can't quite believe it.

Molly laughs. "Oh, Billy," she says.

"She wouldn't pop, though," Polky says. "Tried my best, too." He shrugs. Then he tells us about sneaking her back to town and how

Reese must have been watching from the boat, and that brings him back to tonight. He bangs his fist down on the bar. "Goddamn it," he says. "I should have snapped his goddamn neck."

"No, you shouldn't have," Molly says.

I just sit there, shaking my head. But in a way, it helps. I'm glad we didn't do anything, for sure. Polky and I have a couple more drinks and by the time Molly gives last call, I'm pretty much back to my previous mood. Being drunk definitely helps. When Polky asks for one last shot of schnapps, I say, "Make it two!"

Polky grins at me.

"You two promise you're not driving anywhere?" Molly says.

"Swear to God!" Polky says.

"We're walking," I tell her.

"I trust you, Troy, but I don't trust Billy."

"Cross my heart!" Polky says.

We're the only ones left by this time. The staff has come out to put the chairs upside down on the tables and has been sweeping and cleaning for the past few minutes.

"Give me your keys, then," Molly says.

Polky pulls a tangle of keys out of his pocket. They're on a chain connected to his belt. He disconnects the chain and slaps the keys down on the bar. Molly drops them into her tip jar. They land softly on the cash. "You can come and get them in the morning," she says.

"No problem," Polky says.

We snort our last drinks down, and Polky tucks one more twenty on top of his keys. We say goodnight and stumble over to the door, Polky knocking one of the little tables out of the way, clattering the chairs to the floor. Outside I start off for home, but he says, "Hold on," and fumbles around in his pockets. I wait on the corner: it's quiet, no traffic, nobody around, and it's that after-midnight kind of darkness.

Polky works a key out of his watch pocket and holds it up with a big grin on his face. "Fools 'em every time!" he says. He flips the key up, catches it, flips it again, and I surprise both of us by snatching it out of the air.

He looks at his empty hand. "Hey, give it here!"

"Nope," I say. "You promised."

"You mind your own fucking business!"

I laugh and run across the street. I trip on the curb and nearly fall, but manage to stagger around and keep my feet.

"Goddamn it, Troy!" Polky yells. He comes after me. Being drunk seems to have improved his speed, but I've got the jump on him. I run past the steak house and Erky's wharf and the brass goods place. I sprint along the flat stretch and start up the hill. My legs turn rubbery pretty fast. Then I hear Polky wheezing along behind me. Opposite the yacht club he grabs the back of my shirt and stops me. He lets go and we look at each other, gasping.

"Fork it over!" Polky says between gulps.

"Forget it," I say.

Polky's face turns dark and his big paws clench. "I'm going home and sleep in my own goddamn bed," he says.

I know I ought to hand over the key. There's no traffic and probably the worst that'll happen is that he'll slip on a manhole cover and lose some skin. But I also know Polky doesn't really expect me to give in. Besides, I'm feeling a little ornery myself. I don't like that he lied to Molly. And I guess I'm probably a little jealous.

Polky slugs me behind the ear and I go down, but I get my arms up in time to keep from hitting the pavement face-first. I hear Polky grunt and I roll and he misses diving on me and I hear the "*Oof!*" when he lands. Then we're both on our feet with our fists up. My head is spinning from all the sudden movement. I notice Polky's nose is bleeding and I think he must have been too clumsy to break his own fall. Or maybe I've just pasted him one. I'm not exactly sure.

"God-*damn*, you're an asshole," Polky says.

"Well, you're another," I tell him.

He smirks at that. A fat drop of blood falls out of his nose onto his jacket. Polky tips his head back, sniffing loudly, then spits a big dark clot onto the street. When he smiles at me, his teeth are bloody. "You punk," he says.

I drop my fists and grin.

He feels the edge of his right hand. "You got a hard fucking head."

I notice he used the softer bottom of his fist, and I start to feel sentimental. I'm sorry about hitting him, if that's what I did.

"You're really not gonna give me the key?" Polky says.

"Nope," I say.

He wipes his nose on the back of his hand and says, "Fuck it, then." He slings an arm across my shoulders and we start up the hill. All the houses are dark, and I'm surprised we didn't wake everybody up. Maybe we did and they're hiding under their beds.

"That bitch," Polky says. "That *swank!*"

"She done you wrong," I say.

He claps me on the back and laughs.

THIRTY-ONE

Polky's still asleep when I roll out of bed the next morning. I hear him downstairs, buzzing like a chainsaw. It's nearly seven o'clock, and I've spent the past couple hours too sleepy to get up, but too restless to quite go back to sleep, either. It's always like that when I drink a lot. I go downstairs and past Polky sleeping on the couch. The shades are down, and it's still dark, but I can see that the blanket I gave him is all bunched up around his back and shoulders, and his pale, hairy legs are pulled up like they're trying to crawl back under the covers on their own. I shake my head, thinking about Mallory Reese.

In the kitchen I fire up the Mr. Coffee, and as it coughs and sputters I walk outside. The sun is shining through the tall trees and it looks like a good day to haul, if I wanted to haul. Cool air, warm sun: it's like fall, and reminds me all at once of school buses, of walking down to the corner, of Charlie opening his door and standing there in his undershorts, saying, "Hey there, Troy-boy, do you know if your old man's going out today?"

I drag a chair to a sunny spot on the deck and shut my eyes to the sun. It's cool enough to raise goosebumps, but that won't last long. I open my eyes and watch the shags diving, surfacing to swallow jerkily, their long bills pointed straight up. There's a fish hawk around—I can hear him piping—but he's nowhere in sight. And there are seagulls, as always, looking to get something for nothing.

I go inside for a cup of coffee. Back on the deck I take a couple of sips and my mind clanks into gear and I think: Jesus, tonight's the night. Just like that I get cold feet—I guess I'm too hungover and weak for recklessness. I sit sipping my coffee and the feeling deepens, even though I distinctly remember working it out and deciding I really didn't have a choice.

I'm on my second cup when Polky yells, "God *damn* it!" A minute later he slams the door back and limps out onto the deck. He is quite a sight in undershorts and a black t-shirt with no sleeves. He makes the deck shake, stomping over to the table, drops into a chair, and grabs the toes on his right foot. "I fucking *hate* it when I stub my mother-fucking *little toe!*" he says, his face all squeezed up.

"What'd you hit?" I ask him.

"That goddamn *vacuum* you left in the goddamn *living room!*" He moves his little toe and grimaces. He pushes the toe farther out and makes another pained face.

"Did you break it?" I say.

"No!" He stands up and limps back inside. I hear him kick something, probably the vacuum, probably with the other foot. After a while he comes back out, dressed in jeans, the black t-shirt, and a denim vest. He's still limping, but not as much. He's got his boots on and maybe that helps.

"*Now* I broke your vacuum," he says, "but that's all right, you can buy ten vacuums after tonight."

My stomach rolls over on itself.

"So, you up for some breakfast?" Polky says. He takes a deep fresh-air breath and looks out at the creek and the birds.

"I've got cereal, that's about it."

"Fuck that. Let's go downtown."

In ten minutes we're walking down Seaview Street toward the square. I hear a car horn from somewhere across town and air brakes as a tractor-trailer comes down the grade onto Main Street. There's music playing from an open window: *Midnight at the Oasis*. It's kind of lazy and nice walking down the hill and listening to the song. Then Eddy Cranberry comes out of an alley and shuffles over, long-armed and heavy-browed. "Hey, hey, hey, hey!" he says, like he's excited to see us. He has several days' growth on his cheeks, his hair is matted, and a new pair of overalls rides halfway up his calves.

"Oh, Jesus, I'm gonna puke," Polky says.

But when Eddy comes up even with us—managing to make Polky look small—he isn't all that bad. I realize it must be the new overalls. Eddy gets a pair every few months, and the fresh denim manages to cover up his normal aroma. It's still there underneath, fermenting; but until it busts out he's nearly tolerable.

"Hey, Eddy," I say.

"Hey!"

"Hey, Eddy," Polky drawls.

"Hey!" Eddy says. He has his usual bottle of juice in his big paw. He falls into step with us and we continue on down the hill. We pass a newer, glassy house with a bronze plaque set into its gate that reads, *Harbourlook, 1972*. Then a quick trawl of tourist traps that leads to *The Captain's Table* and the entrance to Erky's wharf. Here Polky says, "Hold on," and tips his head to listen. There's a commotion coming from down by the landing, people laughing and clapping their hands. The sound dies out until somebody yells something and there's more laughter.

"Hartley!" Polky says. "That son of a bitch!"

"Hey!" Eddy says.

Polky looks up at him and says, "Sorry, kid."

"I thought he was all done," I say.

"It's the breakup party," Polky says. "They do it the morning after, before they head out. They invited me, but I never even gave it a thought." He looks at me. "Want to check it out?"

"Not really."

"Oh, come on." He starts off, Eddy falls in behind him, and I sigh and bring up the rear. We walk down the wharf, over the planks set at an angle, like a sergeant's chevron. There are shops on both sides with awnings, big plate-glass windows, and clerks moving around inside. Each store has a wrought-iron bench in front, like a separate little Main Street.

I hear Hartley's gang cooing and clucking as we cut between Erky's office and a place called *The Ice Cream Shoppe*. The tide is dead low, and I can see the granite footings under Danny's pier across the way. The harbor is filling with sailboats, and close by I see the schooner's mast, rigging, and cabin roof. Then I spot the top of the *Julie Marie*'s wheelhouse, and I'm surprised. I forgot about leaving her at the float. I move a little faster to catch up with Polky and Eddy. We pass a girl sitting at a card table on the boardwalk with a poster advertising the schooner's schedule. She sips of her coffee and looks warily at Eddy as we go by. We walk up toward a red, white, and blue *American Road* van nosed into a parking space. The young cop I saw with Lazaro stands by the van with his hands on his gun belt, looking down at the float and smiling like he's enjoying the easy duty.

Eddy Cranberry walks up beside the cop and lets out a grunt. Then Polky says, "What the hell!" and looks back at me.

I catch up and look over the side. There are a lot of people down there, and the party has spread to the other float, and right up onto the *Julie Marie*. There are people actually on my boat, holding coffee cups and pastries, sitting on the rail, standing in the stern. Hartley himself is in the wheelhouse with his arm around some woman and his teeth showing, while a guy on the float takes their picture. Zeiglaar's in the stern, talking to White. Danny Brinker's there, too, nearby on the float.

"I guess they think they already own her," Polky says.

Then Eddy lets out a growl, drops his juice bottle, knocks the young cop out of the way, and charges down the gangway. He's moving pretty fast, because as far as he's concerned, it's *his* goddamn boat they're trespassing on.

The police officer scrambles to his feet and takes off after Eddy. Two guys in gray security uniforms come out from behind the van and go hustling down the gangway, too. They look like a comedy team—one fat, one skinny—and they run holding their phony cop hats on their heads.

It's noisy as hell with all those boots on the aluminum gangway.

Everybody on the first float backs out of Eddy's way, moving behind the catering table with its shiny coffee urn, and Eddy makes it halfway across the walkway before the young cop catches up and grabs his arms. They thrash around, banging and rattling, and Eddy manages to hook a foot around the pipe so the officer can't pull him backwards. The rental cops jitter at the end of the walkway, looking for a chance to get into the mix. It's a stalemate—the young cop must be pretty strong, too—until Charles Reese darts over from the *Julie Marie* and skittishly shoves the toe of Eddy's boot out from under the pipe, which lets the officer stagger backward with Eddy to where the rent-a-cops can pitch in. Then the three of them manage to wrestle Eddy down to the boards, but he's still thrashing like a big old dogfish.

Reese backs up and gives Mallory a triumphant look. That does it for me. I bang down the gangway, with Polky right behind me hollering, "Yee-haw!" At the bottom I try to dodge past the pile of struggling men, but somebody throws out a leg and I trip and fall right onto them. Polky jumps past me and heads for the boat.

Then it seems that everything slows to a crawl. Tangled as I am, I can see Mallory with her hands on her cheeks, Reese snapping his head back and forth, Polky rumbling across the gangway with his hands on the pipes like a big, pissed-off gymnast. I have time to realize that something not all that good is about to happen: Polky has been set free by their trespass on my boat. Then everything speeds up again and I roll clear of Eddy and the cops, catching one big-ass splinter in the palm of my hand in the process. I yank the splinter out and scramble to my feet, just in time to see Polky throw Charles Reese clean off the float. Reese makes a big splash, and almost before he surfaces, Polky has grabbed Mallory, pivoted twice like a dancer whirling his partner, and has thrown *her* over. She flies through the air, all arms and legs, and there's a shriek and another splash. The two of them tread water, gasping. I'm frozen, watching. Polky looks at Taylor Miles, who says, "I'm sorry," and stands there like he's resigned to going in the drink with the rest of them. Danny is behind Taylor Miles, cowering, looking at me.

"Hey!" Eddy yells, and I turn to see Eddy with his face mashed into the planks and the three law enforcement dudes still working violently to get the cuffs on him. I jump back, yank the first one I can reach off of him and sling him out of the way. It's the skinny security guy, and he trips over a cleat and nearly goes into the water.

"You keep out of this!" the young cop yells from his knees. He's lost his beret and his bright red hair is all over the place. He's got his handcuffs out and is trying with the second security guy—who has Eddy in a headlock—to get them onto Eddy's wrists. But Eddy's still bucking and flopping, making it nearly impossible.

"I'm warning you," the red-headed officer says to me. He pushes his shoulder down against Eddy's back, hanging on to his arm, trying to bend it into place for the cuffs.

"God damn it!" Donald Hartley roars then from the boat. "Has everybody in this town gone crazy?"

Several things happen at once: Eddy hears Hartley swear and snaps his head up from the planks; the red-headed officer shifts position, trying for a better angle, and Hartley lets out a second "God *damn* it, people!" just as I grab the fat security guy and pull him backwards. This frees Eddy for a split-second, long enough to jackknife to his feet, shove the cops away—the red-head trips and bangs his head hard on the planks—and charge across the walkway toward the man who's just taken the Lord's name in vain, twice. Hartley's eyes get big watching Eddy lumber toward him with his giant hands out. When Eddy starts to climb over the rail, Hartley and the woman he was posing with sprint out of the wheelhouse and jump off the stern. There's a loud, plunging, double splash and they surface, gasping at the coldness of the water. The woman's *American Road* hat floats away.

Eddy gets both feet on the *Julie Marie*'s deck and starts after Zeiglaar and White, who don't hesitate to follow Hartley's example. More splashes and gasps follow. Then I run up and Danny goes off the far side of the float, making the smallest splash so far.

Eddy stops at the transom—he can't swim.

By now the red-head officer has recovered and made it over to the second float with his pistol drawn. "That's enough, all of you!" he shouts. He points with his free hand at me and says, "Back off!" then looks over at Polky, standing next to Taylor Miles, and says, "Cease and desist!" Then he looks at Eddy Cranberry on the boat and says, "You make a goddamn move and I'll blow your fucking head off!"

Eddy Cranberry's eyes narrow, he takes two steps and climbs out of the boat. The officer backs up a step and shakes the pistol. "I'm not kidding!"

"Be cool, Eddy!" I yell.

Eddy stops and looks at me, ugly as hell. His overall straps are down and his t-shirt torn so that one big, muscular shoulder shows through. It's slick with sweat and dirt.

"I mean it," I tell Eddy.

He sneers, but doesn't move.

The officer points the gun at me, then back at Eddy. Then he points it at Polky and back at Eddy. For a second everything holds still. I have this realization that it's a beautiful spring day, the sun is shining, the water's sparkling, and there's a cop pointing a gun around to stop a rumble while Donald Hartley and his gang tread water and try not to freeze.

Polky looks at me and grins.

Then Trace White shouts, "*Do* something, you idiot, I'm cramping!" and when the startled cop looks his way, Eddy lunges and sinks a big fist about six inches into his gut. The officer drops his pistol and bends double, and Eddy brings the other fist down onto the back of his head like a sledgehammer.

THIRTY-TWO

As we approach Shag Island I look over my shoulder, sighting past the *Julie Marie*'s wake toward the landing. It's still plenty hectic. I guess that's what happens when you put Donald Hartley of *American Road* and several of his associates over the side, and for good measure beat up his security detail.

Polky looks sideways at me, like a kid trying not to laugh.

I just shake my head. I'm wondering if we should have stayed and faced the music. But people were hollering for someone to call 911, the red-headed cop was stretched out cold, or maybe even dead, and it was probably just as well to leave the scene. Not that we really thought things through. We jumped aboard and Polky shook the lines free, and nobody tried to interfere with us, not even the rental cops. I fired up the engine and we blasted the hell out of there.

"Fuck it," I say now, above the noisy engine.

"Fuck it!" Polky sings out.

I steer us between the end of the point and Shag Island and take another look back at the landing. There are still no blue lights anywhere.

"They had it coming, crawling around on your boat," Polky yells.

"That's right," I say. "They don't own her yet!"

"They ain't *going* to own her!"

"Hey!" Eddy shouts from his seat on the engine hatch.

It's all bravado, though: I'm worried as hell. But still I notice how it's coming on beautiful on the water, with the sun high up over the islands, and how the trees ashore are swaying, big and leafy. On our port side the point falls away and I can see all of The Havens and Big Branch, and way out beyond, the two peaks of Mt. Desert Island.

I steer on down the bay.

"So where are we going?" Polky yells.

"You got me," I yell back.

"They'll come after us."

"No shit."

"Did you see the look on old Zeagull's face?" Polky looks back at Eddy—the slipstream flipping his matted hair around—and gives him the thumbs-up. Eddy tries to imitate him, but ends up looking more like somebody ringing a doorbell.

We skip along, raising a splashy fan on each side.

"They won't arrest Eddy," Polky says. "He ain't responsible for himself."

"What about us?" I say.

"We're fucked!"

I take us toward Owls Head, laughing.

"You could park her at the pound," Polky says. "Get a ride back to Pequot. Come get her after things simmer down. Who would be home in the middle of the goddamn day?"

"Bobby Lawson might," I say.

"I thought he hated you."

"Naw, we talked it out."

"Ain't that sweet."

I slow the *Julie Marie* and swing her around in a circle so I can take one last look toward the landing. The blue lights are there, finally. We cross our own wake, skipping and bumping. But that only lasts a few seconds, and then I feed her the gas and we steam along on our new course.

We ride parallel to the Rockland Breakwater and on across the outer harbor, rounding the point with the lighthouse, crossing the Owls Head harbor mouth, and leaving it behind. The shoreline drops away and we follow it out past the Number Two Point until the big, curved beach blooms up ahead. I steer past Bobby's cabin, toward his old brown dock, and ease off on the power. We settle in the water and run up slow. Bobby hears us coming and walks out of the cabin, tucking in his long-john shirt. I cut the engine and Bobby calls out, "What's up?" as we drift close. I toss him the line and we join him on the dock, where I give him the short version of our little adventure at the landing.

Bobby's eyes get wide. "Donald Hartley?" he says.

"Afraid so," I say.

"God-*damn!*"

"Hey!" Eddy glowers down at Bobby.

"Sorry, Eddy," Bobby says, holding up his hands.

"Anyway," I say, "if I put my boat over to the pound do you think you could you run us back to town?"

"Sure, if we'll all fit in my truck."

"I'll ride in the back," Polky says.

"No way," Bobby says. "Eddy rides in the back. No offense, Eddy."

Eddy's looking out at the water, not listening.

"He ain't real bad today," Polky says.

"I still want him in the back," Bobby says. Then he grabs me by the arm. "Why not leave her right here?"

"You wouldn't mind?"

"Naw! Come on. I'll run you back."

We walk around the cabin to his backyard, past the dilapidated wooden boat, past his dead stock car, to his driveway. He's got a pickup that's even older than mine. There's a sheet of half-inch plywood covering up the holes in the load bed. Bobby drops the tailgate and Eddy climbs in, moves some rope into place for a pillow, and lies down on his back with his legs crossed. He stares up at the trees. For a second he looks halfway normal.

"You okay?" I ask him.

Eddy nods, still looking up at the trees.

Polky and I squeeze into the front seat with Bobby. It takes

Polky three tries to pull the door shut against his hip. Bobby cranks the engine, stomps the gas pedal, cranks it again, and this time it catches and we set off banging over the dirt driveway.

"I can't believe you guys," Bobby says.

"Neither could they," Polky says.

We ride down to the main road and head back around Rockland. Both windows are open: it's warm out now. Bobby takes the back way to Pequot, past Chickawaukee Lake. I see they've got their floats in already for summer. One even has a diving board. We ride between high hills with rock faces, skirt another couple of ponds, and run into Pequot along Mechanic Street. Bobby cuts across to Main and double-parks by the flagpole, goosing the engine to keep it from stalling. Polky and I squeeze out and Eddy crawls out of the back. We all stand there on the grass.

"Thanks, man," I say to Bobby.

"Don't mention it." Bobby gives a little salute, looks over his shoulder, and steers out into the traffic. He runs down to Chestnut and hangs a right, disappearing behind the church, grinding his gears, heading back to Owls Head.

"Hey!" Eddy's hand is out.

Polky digs into his pocket and slaps a bill into his hand. "Here you go, Eddy. You done good."

Eddy sticks his fist into his pocket and marches up Main Street toward the boarding home in the old elementary school building. Polky and I start across the green toward the church.

"We're still on for tonight, right?" Polky says.

"I'll be there," I say. It's not like I have any choice, after this morning. But that's all right. I didn't have any choice before. I'm over my hangover weakness. It makes me feel good not having a choice. Kind of like being down ten with a minute to go and knowing the pressure's off, so you might as well start firing up the threes.

"So, midnight."

"Old fire station," I say.

Polky's new hairdo is gone. The run across the bay blew it away, and he's back to looking like a pirate, a pirate with a big grin on his face. "What are you going to do now?" he says.

"Sneak home and get my pickup."

"Don't get caught," Polky says. He salutes me like Bobby did and heads off for his bike, parked near the post office. He's swiveling his head around, looking for trouble. I cross the green and take the path that goes through the dusty bushes to Seaview Street. At Seaview I look past the yacht club at the water dancing in the sunlight, and I picture Hartley and Keith and the Reeses splashing around, and the red-headed cop dropping like he'd been shot. I walk a little faster up the hill.

THIRTY-THREE

At the top of Seaview I trot over to the harbor bank and down into the shadows under the bridge. There's trash all the way down: fast-food wrappers and oil containers, a piece of somebody's tire, and a rusty section of exhaust pipe. I reach the water and step from rock to rock around the corner from harbor to creek and along the creek bank below Charlie Hamalainen's, pushing through bushes where there aren't any steppingstones. It takes me fifteen minutes to get to my house. I start up over the bank, but hit the deck when the shags take off suddenly: first a couple, then ten, then the whole mass clattering into the air, the noise doubling and tripling as they launch away over the trees. I lie on the dead sticks and leaves until I can hear again. Then I creep up to the big ash at the edge of my lawn. I peek around the tree and see Niki's car in the driveway, then Niki herself coming up the path with her quick walk, dressed for work in a tan skirt and jacket.

She climbs the steps and knocks at the door. Then she opens the door and goes right in. After a minute or two she's back, jogging down the steps and over to her car. When she drives off I cross to the house, go upstairs and dig the .357 out from under my mattress. I heft it, then change my mind and tuck it back. Driving around with a loaded firearm is probably not the smartest move just now. I run outside and jump in the pickup. I drive down the hill, take the side street past the P.O., hang a left, and head the back way into Rockland. It's only eleven-thirty and I've decided to go to Gary's. Polky and I never did get breakfast, and nobody would look for me there. I imagine it's a foregone conclusion that they're looking for me. Hell, it's probably been on the news by now: *American Road Host Attacked During Cast Party!*

What the hell, I think. A last meal.

At Gary's, Sandy comes up and says, "What on earth did you guys do?" She has ketchup stains on her blue uniform and a stub of a pencil behind her ear.

"When?" I say.

"When you beat up Donald Hartley!"

"We never touched Donald Hartley."

"That's not what they're saying on the TV." She leans across the counter. "Anybody who sees you is supposed to call the police, Troy."

I look the place over: folks eating the meatloaf special, drinking coffee, smoking. Nobody seems to be paying me any attention, but I decide I'd probably better keep Sandy and Gary out of it. "Well, how about making me a couple of sandwiches?" I say.

"You bet." She sounds relieved.

"Five of them," I say. "You got any crabmeat?"

She runs off, hustles back with a paper bag stuffed with sandwiches, cookies, and potato chips.

"What do I owe you?"

"You can settle up later."

I thank her and take the sandwiches outside. I drive out into the sticks, and after a mile of woods road, turn onto a weedy track, where I bump along to the end and park. I walk down the path to the little cove and balance along the planks toward Bobby's, looking through the tall white pines at the *Julie Marie* tied up to his dock, framed by the blue water.

Bobby's cabin door opens and I stop.

Officer Tracy Thibeault comes strutting out onto the porch, holding her gun in both hands. She's got a look on her face like a Roman emperor about to turn the old thumb down. "Hands up," she says to me.

Right behind her is Bobby Lawson, looking upset.

"Aw, man," Bobby says. "Old Dickless here spotted your boat. Put ashore up on the sand so you wouldn't see. Came in and took us all hostage."

"Sir, go back inside, or you'll be joining your friend," Thibeault says.

Bobby waves disgustedly and goes back inside.

When the door shuts, Thibeault says, "Mr. Hull, please turn around and put your hands behind you." She steps down off the porch, feeling with her feet, the pistol wobbling a bit in her small hands. I see Bobby's kids at the windows. Thibeault keeps the gun trained on me with one hand while she works a pair of handcuffs off her belt with the other.

"Oh yeah," I say. "Don't forget the cuffs."

"Turn around, put the paper bag down, and put your hands behind your back," Thibeault says.

I drop the bag, turn with my hands behind me, and after a moment I feel the warm metal snap around my wrists. She ratchets it up pretty tight.

THIRTY-FOUR

It takes twenty minutes for Chief Lazaro to show up, and the whole time Dickless Tracy keeps me sitting on the swampy grass. When we finally hear the cruiser she wags her head for me to get to my feet, and marches me around the house to Bobby's driveway. At the backed-in cruiser she pushes my head down and shoves me into the back seat. Then she slams the door and gets in front with the chief.

It's uncomfortable, sitting there with a wet ass.

"Well, well," the chief says. He smiles over his shoulder and nods. The beret goes up and down. Thibeault grins at me, too.

"You guys ought to swap hats," I say.

Lazaro's jaw clenches. He puts the cruiser in gear and takes us out onto the dusty dirt road.

"You're a real riot," Thibeault says.

I don't say anything more. Nobody says anything the rest of the way to the county jail, next to the four-story brick courthouse, a block away from Main Street in Rockland.

The jail is brick, too, with a row of identical cells along one side with barred windows, a bunk, and a vile-looking toilet. I sit on the cot trying to decide who might be willing to bail me out. I called the bail bondsman—the old officer at the front desk gave me his number—but the guy wasn't home. The old cop offered me another chance, and I told him I had to think about it, and I'm still thinking. They'd bust Polky the minute he walked in. Bobby Lawson wouldn't have any money. Stewie Lapinen would, but it doesn't seem right to ask a friend of the old man's. It doesn't feel right to call Niki, either.

She doesn't need to be mixed up with Knox County's public enemy number one.

I was charged with assault and interfering with a police officer, and the officer said I was lucky the red-head hadn't ruptured something or get a concussion or the lot of us would probably be up for felony assault on an officer. This old cop had white hair, deep bags under his eyes, and a tiny, sad mouth. He pushed a form across the desk and said, "Sign here." I signed, then asked about filing a complaint of my own for trespass. He told me to do it after I got out. "It's not anything we'd chase anybody down for," he said. Then he led me through a locked metal shutdown door to the cells.

I look around at the graffiti on the walls. Penises seem to be popular, some with little faces and word balloons. One of them says *Chief Lazaro sucks donkey dicks!!!*

My stomach growls and I think of the crab rolls.

I wonder how the bail bondsman can be so out of touch? Maybe they figure it's a good thing to let criminals like me stew for a while. I stew for another hour in the cramped little cell, and have almost decided to use the toilet when the old-timer comes limping down the corridor with a big key ring in his hand. He walks up and struggles to unlock my cage. I walk over and hold onto the metal bars.

Finally he manages to open the door. "Come on out," he says. "You're free to go."

"How'd that happen?" I say.

He just nods toward the front. We go back out and he ushers me into the lobby, where Niki Harjula sits waiting on a wooden bench. She puts her hands on her knees and rises as we enter the room. She's still wearing her work outfit, and she's looking pretty solemn.

"Niki," I say. "You paid my bail?"

"Uh-huh," she says.

"You shouldn't have done that."

"Well, I did."

"Let's not get ahead of ourselves." The old officer takes a big yellow envelope from a drawer and empties it onto his desk. "Please verify that all your possessions have been returned to you and sign the form at the bottom," he says, and puts a clipboard beside my wallet. I sign the form, put my wallet in my pocket, my watch on my wrist, my belt through the loops on my pants. I stick the shoelaces in my pocket.

"Keep your nose clean, now." He looks at me with his little mouth closed up tight.

Niki takes my hand. Outside the sun is low over town, and the parking lot is in shadow, but I'm surprised it's still daylight, the same way you're surprised coming out of a matinee. Niki opens her door and looks over the little car's roof at me before she gets in. I lower myself onto the passenger seat and say, "How'd you get out of work?"

She just shakes her head.

"What?" I say.

She holds a finger up, backs out of the parking spot, and crosses a side street to Main. The VW sounds like a lawn mower from the inside, and my knees feel like they're up around my chin. Niki drives like a girl, hands at ten and two. We follow Route 1 through the Rockland downtown, stopping at the light opposite the movie theater. The light changes, we drive past the ferry terminal and up the fast-food stretch, past a MacDonald's, a Burger King, a Denny's.

My stomach growls. Niki slows down and looks at me.

"I'll wait," I say. "Tell me what's going on."

She speeds up as we leave Rockland behind, driving with both hands on the wheel, sitting upright. When we cruise through the green light by Wal-Mart she nods her head and says, "After I heard what happened I went over to see you. You weren't home, though. When I got back to the bank, Keith wanted to know where I'd been, and when I told him he gave me a whole bunch of grief."

"Why even tell him?" I say.

"I don't need to lie to people like that."

We pass the maple syrup place, the hearing aid place with the giant ear sign, the farm store, all on the left. There's nothing on the right but woods. Niki stares at the road as she drives.

"So how'd he take it?"

"He said he was starting to wonder where my loyalties were. That's when I told him he was a fine one to talk about loyalties."

We ride past Pequot Sports, kayaks and canoes stacked around its little home-made pond. She says, "He told me I was upset and should take the rest of the day off, and while I was at it maybe I should think about working for someone I held in such low esteem. I said I didn't need a whole day to figure that one out, and he said, "Fine, then."

I don't know what to say.

Niki steers through the light and down to the square. The sidewalks are pretty busy, like the season's really under way. I look at the drugstore and half expect Mallory Reese to come walking out. But no Mallory. Niki hangs a hard right onto Seaview Street and we ride past the shops on the flat stretch and start up the hill through the shadows.

"So what were you guys thinking, anyway?" Niki says.

"It's a long story."

"I've got the time," she says.

So as we ride up the hill, I tell how Eddy Cranberry led the charge and how it just unfolded after that. I describe Eddy knocking the red-headed cop out and us running for it in the *Julie Marie.* I tell her about Dickless Tracy hiding in Bobby Lawson's house and busting me.

She turns onto Hull Street. I see that somebody has been up here with a mower: there are three-foot-wide strips on both shoulders, the cut grass already turning yellow. We pull into the driveway and Niki shuts off the engine and sits with her hands in her lap. She looks at me and shakes her head like she can't believe what's happened, and then all of a sudden puts her face in her hands. A sob sneaks out of her, but she clamps down tight before she actually starts crying. I don't think I've ever heard her cry. I remember when she was little she fell on the street once and scraped the skin off her knees. Even that didn't make her cry.

I put my arm around her and gather her in. She turns her face to my chest. Then she clenches her fists and presses them against her temples. I feel helpless, but after a little while manage to figure out that I should take her inside. I reach past her and open the door. "Let's go in," I say. I get out, circle the car, and put my arm around her as we walk to the deck, up the steps, and into the house. In the living room she clutches her stomach and says, "Oh, Troy, I feel sick."

I take her arm, walk her into the big bedroom. The bed is still made up with our old bedspread. I've left it alone. Every now and then I shake the dust off it.

"Curl up here," I say. "I'll get you a drink."

"I'm not thirsty," she says, and looks up at me with big, wet eyes. Then she turns her eyes down. I sit next to her and say, "This is all my goddamn fault."

She takes a deep breath with a hitch in it.

I pull the bedspread back and ease her over and lie down next to her. I flap the bedspread back over us and put my arms around her. Even then it takes a while before she lets go, but when she does it's like a dam busting. She sobs and gasps for breath. It's like holding a broken-hearted little kid, all her grownup-ness cried away. I stroke her hair until it eases up and she begins to relax. After a couple of big, shaky breaths she opens her eyes, looks at me, then just drops off to sleep. I hold her and listen to her breathe, and now I'm kind of turned on, so for a while have to keep a little separation between us so I won't poke her. I smirk at myself and then start to drift off, too. It's been a wicked long day. I turn my head so I'm not breathing into her face, and I shut my eyes and follow her all the way down.

THIRTY-FIVE

I'm standing on the creek bank, smoking a cigarette, looking downstream at the crescent moon sitting just over the trees behind the bridge, on the other side of the harbor. I've been mooning around since Niki left an hour ago. We slept for quite a while, and when I woke it was dim in the room and I was confused to be there. Niki was standing beside the bed and it took me a moment to realize what she was doing in my house. Then I remembered, and I remembered some other things, too, as I watched her smoothing her clothes in front of the vanity mirror, in the weak leftover daylight from the window.

"Going somewhere?" I said from the bed.

She turned her head. "To clean out my desk while I still have a key."

"I'm wicked sorry, Niki."

"It's okay. I'm sorry I was such a baby."

"I didn't mind," I said.

She looked at me for a moment, then turned back to the mirror and tugged at her jacket. She was being very efficient, no-nonsense.

"What are you going to do afterward?" I said.

"I don't know."

I tried to sit up, but my back was too stiff. I wasn't used to sleeping with someone in my arms. I had to roll onto my side, push myself up that way. "You can come back here, if you want," I said with the covers around my waist.

She gave me the look again.

"I mean, I'd like you to," I said.

She came over and sat on the bed, half-smiling. Her face was all planes and angles in the thin light. She brushed a hand through her hair and looked at me. I took her hands, remembered holding her and going to sleep, remembered kissing her sleepily sometime later. I definitely remembered a light coming on in my poor foggy head.

"Troy, honest, you don't owe me—"

"If you say that again I will kick your ass," I said, and tugged her down beside me. She let me kiss her. After a while she opened her eyes. "Us?" she said. "When did that happen?"

"Tonight."

Her face was inches from mine. "Really?"

"Yeah, I'm a little slow."

She closed her eyes and we kissed for a long time. The side of her face fit my palm perfectly. She opened her eyes and let me see all the way into them. "Okay, but don't you dare break my heart," she said with a little laugh. I felt again what I'd felt earlier, waking with her in my arms, and then I thought about her coming back and the two of us sleeping together tonight.

That's when I remembered Polky.

"Niki," I said. "Listen, if I'm gone when you get back, come in and wait for me. Don't let that change anything."

"Where are you going?"

For a moment I thought about lying. "I have to meet Polky," I said.

She pulled back her head an inch or two and stared.

"I'm sorry," I said.

"I don't want you to go. Not now."

"I can't back out this late," I said.

"Yes you can."

"I won't," I said, after a second.

"What if something happens?"

"Nothing will happen."

"You know better than that," she said. "Something always happens to people like us."

"I'll be careful."

"This isn't fair, Troy Hull. Not one bit."

"I'm sorry," I said. "It was before I knew."

She threw back the bedspread and got out of the bed, gave me a last ferocious look, and walked out of the room. I heard the door slide shut, and I heard her drive off fast. I got up and washed my face in the kitchen sink and went outside and smoked a cigarette and thought hard about it. But I couldn't talk myself out of going. I'd promised, and besides, I still didn't feel like I had any choice. I walked down off the deck and wandered around the property and smoked another cigarette and gave myself plenty of time, but nothing I thought of managed to change my mind.

Now I turn my wrist to look at the time. It's nearly eleven o'clock, and I need to think about getting my ass in gear. I look up at the stars, stalling just a little longer, picking out constellations without knowing their names. I toss my cigarette into the creek and turn to go. My heart beats faster. Niki or no Niki, I'm still ready to start firing up the threes. The cool air drifts over my face and I hear peepers from the little bog. I can smell the brackish water. I walk back to the house and retrieve the .357 from under my mattress, and this time I carry it out to the truck. I drive down to the five-way and back through town, stopping long enough to run into the convenience store opposite the plaza and buy a pack of Polky's little cigars. Then I head out of town.

THIRTY-SIX

I sit in my pickup, hidden behind the old, boarded-up brick firehouse at the intersection of 17 and 90. The sky is still littered with stars, but the moon is gone and it is dark and quiet. I've been puffing on one of the little cigars, the window cracked. Polky's half an hour late. I pitch the cigar stub into the grass and wonder if something's gone wrong. There must be a lot that can go wrong with a deal like this. For a moment I almost hope he doesn't show, but then I remember I'll probably lose my house if this doesn't work out.

I hear a car coming. The car approaches fast, barrels through the intersection without even slowing. Then it's quiet again. I turn the radio on and listen to Rockland's country station until another vehicle comes down the road. I shut the radio off and watch headlights playing on the stop sign. The dome light comes on and Polky grins out the window. The dome light goes off and the pickup heads down 17, around a corner and out of sight.

I take off after him, and pretty soon I can see him again, just cruising along. We ride over a series of low hills and past a couple of ponds. There are solitary houses every mile or two, some with corrals. I keep the window down for the fresh air, not that there's any real danger of getting sleepy, and we pass the trading post with the Indian statue next to its gas pumps, then another pond shining in the starlight. We run another two or three miles through the countryside and come up to a crossroads. Polky's blinker goes on once, and he pulls into the parking lot of a long, jointed wooden garage. There are five bay doors in a row, and a light on over the office door even though the place is shut down. I can read the hand-painted sign: KIMBALL'S BODY REPAIR, and I remember the old guy we'd bribe to sell us stickers for our jalopies.

I go past the garage and turn left at a four way. This road curves up a hill behind the garage and when I get to the shack Polky mentioned, I poke the lights off and drive around it to park in the shadows. I'm nervous, but still not all that scared. There aren't any police departments out here, maybe two deputies on patrol in the whole county, and any state trooper in the neighborhood is most likely eating pie at Moody's Diner ten miles away.

I pull the seat lever and shove back to get a little more room behind the wheel.

"*OW!*" comes from behind me.

My heart nearly jumps out of my mouth, but in that same instant I know whose voice it is, and I pull the seat forward again and look back at Niki Harjula, all scrunched up in the extended-cab, rubbing her head, looking embarrassed and about eight years old. She laughs and squirms over the top of the seat into the front. "I was doing okay until you pushed the seat back," she says. She's wearing jeans and a dark blouse, and I figure she went home to change before going to the office.

"Niki," I say. "You stowed away?"

"I'm sorry," she says. "I came out of the bank and saw your pickup. It made me mad all over again. I walked over and when you came out of the store I just opened the door and jumped right in and hid without even thinking about it."

"I never saw you."

"I was behind the pumps," she says, "and you were busy opening your little cigar pack." She looks at me, chin up. "So here I am, Troy Hull." She holds a hand up. "Don't bother trying to do anything about it. I won't ask you to leave because I know you promised. But I'm staying, too." She gives me the stubborn look I've known since we were little kids. I realize it's too late to do anything with her anyway. If I leave now, I'm liable to scare Polky's customer away.

"All right," I say.

She scootches over and takes my hand in both of hers. She kisses my hand and looks at me and I feel happiness rise in me. Then I remember what's going on and I look down the hill toward the garage. But nothing's happening yet.

"So what are we doing?" Niki says.

"Nothing. Waiting here until they're done, going home."

About two minutes later headlights come over the hill behind us and a small car passes our hiding place and proceeds down the road toward the garage. The car turns into the lot and goes out of sight, but then I see its beams reaching past the other end of the garage.

"Is that them?" Niki whispers.

"I think so."

The headlights seem to brighten, and then blink out. There's still enough light from the front to see the car move around the corner of the building, turn almost to the edge of the lot, and circle back to Polky's truck. I'm still not scared, really, even with Niki here. It's like a fire drill: you never think there's going to be an actual fire. Polky and his clients will do their business and we'll go home and pick up where we left off.

But then the fire drill turns real.

Another car comes speeding down 17, slowing as it reaches the garage, and I get a bad feeling. But Polky doesn't throw his headlights on, which is supposed to be our distress signal. I stick my head out the window and listen to tires popping over the rubble where the pavement is broken up. I see the second car move around the corner of the garage.

Now Polky's lights go on and his engine cranks. And all hell breaks loose. The first car squeals straight back past the second car. There's a *pop pop pop* that sounds like firecrackers, and flashes in the dark, and then the first car fishtails away through the intersection and off down the road. The second car swings sideways to block

Polky and somebody gets out, runs over, and fires a couple more quick shots at Polky. A wounded howl shocks me into action. I yell, "Hit the deck," and shove Niki down, then set off bouncing down the overgrown cart path. I fire three rounds out the window into the air, and the shadow hurries back to its car and the car skids around the corner, squealing onto the road and burning away north. I slam on my brakes, snatch the flashlight from my glove box, say, "Stay here!" to Niki, and kick the door open. Broken glass crunches under my boots and sparkles in the beam of the flashlight. I duck up to the pickup and aim the light in, scared at what I might see. But Polky is still breathing, at least. His eyes are squeezed shut like he's waiting for somebody to finish him off, and when it doesn't happen he opens them and squints into the light. I turn it on myself and he says, "Jesus! it's about time!"

"How bad did they get you?" I say.

Polky groans. He's holding onto his side, the big claw all bloody. The side of his head is bloody, too: I shine the light on it and see they shot a piece of his ear off. Blood is running down into his beard.

"Can you get out?" I say. "I'll take you to the hospital."

"No!" Polky says. "The *stuff* is still here. On the floor."

I shine the light on a small duffle bag.

Polky twists suddenly and grunts with pain.

"I've got to take you in," I say.

"I'm not going to jail, Troy!"

I hear a siren in the distance then, and the hair on my neck bristles.

"Take it and go!" Polky groans. "Hide it somewhere!"

"Are you sure?"

"Go!"

I lean in and grab the bag. It's heavy, soft.

The siren comes closer.

I lift the bag out through the window and run back to my pickup. I throw it in the back, jump in, slam the door. My hand shakes turning the key. Niki looks at me but doesn't say anything. I spin the steering wheel, drive around the garage just as two sets of blue lights come out of the long curve to the straightaway leading to Kimball's Garage. I circle left, running with my lights off, and accelerate as fast as I can without squealing. I run up the hill along the Seven Tree Pond Road, leaning close to the steering wheel, straining to see down the narrow road. After a minute or two I think we might be in the clear. But then I see the blue lights behind us.

"Damn it!" I say.

Niki looks over her shoulder. "Should we stop?

"No," I say, and I drive on, trying to think, my mind racing. I could pull into someone's driveway and we could duck down, but that seems like a fool's plan. Cops know their business better than that. What else can I do? I could toss the stuff out the window, except I threw it in the back and can't reach it. If I stop to retrieve it, then set off again, they'll catch me, and even if I manage to ditch the duffle, they'll just backtrack and find it, no problem. Of course, then they'd have to prove that I'm the one who threw it out. There's that.

I drive by starlight and the faint glow from roadside houses, trying not to drift too close to either side of the road. Niki has moved over and put her seatbelt on. I'm trying to figure the odds of beating the rap, when I remember our old camp. It's not all that far from here.

A quarter mile on I turn onto a side road and goose it down a long hill, checking my rear-view mirror, seeing the cruiser take the same turnoff. He's making up ground pretty fast. I speed down a straight stretch, follow a long turn to the left, the truck rattling and shaking. When I come out of the turn, I pull my lights on—I've got cover for the next thirty seconds or so. I look for a break in the line of trees. It's been a few years, but I remember it's close by a big old chestnut.

I spot the chestnut and slow quickly to turn onto a two-rut woods road, poking the lights off and crunching over sticks and dirt, following the woods road down the hill and stopping. I look over my shoulder and see the cruiser come over the last rise and race along the road past my turnoff. When he's gone I pull my parking lights on and go the rest of the way down to the lake, branches scratching across the doors. I take a moment to hope Polky will be okay, then think suddenly about my parents, grandparents, uncles, aunts, cousins. Polky and Niki, too, all sitting at a picnic table, eating lobster, corn on the cob, hamburgers, hotdogs, potato salad, watermelon. I remember taking canoes and rowboats out on the lake, sleeping on cots set up with thick green army blankets and canvas pillows. I remember fishing poles in the shed and an old iron basketball rim nailed to a tree without a backboard.

Niki says, "Oh!" and looks out the window as we bump along into the camp's driveway. I stop and shut off the engine. We roll the windows down and listen. The camp is dark and quiet. I don't even know who owns the place any more. I hear waves rolling gently against the shore. Across the lake are lights, small and white in the distance, their reflections wavy in the water. I make sure my dome light is off, open the door, and get out. Niki chunks her door shut. I see blue light again, coming slowly back our way.

"What now?" Niki says.

I drum my fingers on the roof, look around. If I just scatter it on the ground, they'll find traces. If I dump it in the lake it'll clump together and wash ashore. If I bury it they'll bring a dog and dig it up.

The cruiser is moving downhill, checking another access road. I scan the lake, where it narrows off to our left, and then I look at the old rusty hoop on the pine next to the camp. My fingers tap once on the pickup's roof, and then I yank open the door and lean over the seat to grab the basketball. I dig my jackknife out, and moving fast, cut a slit in the ball. The air puffs out and I take the zip-locks out of the duffle and stuff them in.

"What are you doing?" Niki says.

"Getting rid of this."

I find an EZ-ON tire patch in my tool chest, peel the backing off and smooth the tacky side against the worn-down pebbles of the basketball. Then I snap my lighter open and, hiding the light behind the pickup, heat the patch. After a couple of minutes I take the hand pump from my tool chest and refill the ball, leaving it a little soft so as not to blow out the patch.

"Come on," I say, and I run down to the lake, Niki close behind. The water is silvery up close, like it's soaking in the starlight and holding it just under the surface. We crunch along a gravel beach and turn onto a path into the woods that leads us to an earthen berm. There's a rushing sound, the water skimming into what's left of the old canal. I plant a kiss on the patch and ease the basketball into the water, and it floats away, riding low. I take the .357 out of my pocket, grip it by the barrel and throw it as far as I can out into the canal. There's a little *bloop* when it hits the water.

We run back. When we get to the beach I see the cruiser's lights up near the blacktop. We trot over to the pickup and climb in and turn to watch him slowly head our way. Now there's nothing we can do but sit in the dark and wait.

"Oh God, I *hate* this," Niki whispers.

"I'm not too fond of it myself."

She looks at me, and I can feel the question.

"Yeah," I say. "If we get out of this, I'm through with it."

"Promise?"

"Yeah."

"Good," Niki says. She looks over her shoulder. "Coast down a little closer, Troy."

She's unbuttoning her blouse.

"Go on," she says.

I push in the clutch and let the pickup drift a few yards closer to the lake. I stop it with the parking brake. Niki finishes with her blouse, shrugs it out of the way and reaches up between her breasts to unsnap her bra. She messes up her hair with her hands and leans against me. "Kiss me," she says, and she takes my hand and places it on her breast. Then I'm lost in her lips and the warm, small heft of her and the little sound she makes in the back of her throat. I don't even hear the cruiser come into the driveway behind us. We kiss until the flashlight beam breaks into our space, and then Niki jumps and turns away, snatching her bra back into place, and I squint into the light, as irritated as if I hadn't known it was coming.

"Evenin'," the state trooper says. He cocks his head to look in the window, a tall guy with a narrow face and a deep voice. "Driver's license and registration, please?"

"Could you turn that light away for a minute?"

"No sir, sorry." He keeps it shining into the pickup, while I lean past Niki and dig the paperwork out of the glove box. Her fingers are moving up the blouse, quick and nimble. The trooper takes the papers, shines the light on them briefly, then aims the light behind me and sweeps it around that space.

"Something wrong?" I say.

Niki finishes with her blouse and sits with her head down.

"Chasin' somebody," the state trooper says. "Thought they might've come down this way. Excuse me a minute." He walks back to his cruiser. Pretty quickly he's back, handing me my paperwork, walking around to the front of the pickup to put his hand on the hood. "Been here long?" he says.

"Just a little while." I look at Niki. "You all right?"

"No," she says. "I want to go home."

"I'm sorry," I say.

"Just take me home, please." She's sitting with her legs crossed now, hugging herself.

I look up at the trooper.

"Sorry," he says, "I just need to take a better look inside. If you wouldn't mind." He steps back. We get out and he leans into the pickup, looks under the seats, the glove box, checks the door pockets and the visors and the extended cab space again. He backs out and kneels to look underneath, stands up and examines the loadbed and my toolbox. Then he shuts the flashlight off and says, "Sorry to have bothered you folks, but there was some excitement tonight and I had to check you out."

"All right," I say.

He nods toward the camp. "This *is* private property."

"We weren't hurting anything."

"You probably want to head out of here anyway. Why don't you follow me up to the road and then go on home?" He touches his trooper hat, says, "Ma'am," and heads back to the cruiser. We follow him up to the road and when he turns right, I go left and drive to Waldoboro and come back on Route 1, through Thomaston and Rockland. It's dark and quiet, the middle of the night, without much traffic.

"I guess it's a good thing you stowed away," I tell Niki.

"It doesn't feel very good," she says.

I put my hand on her knee, and after a moment she covers it with her own. We take the back way to Pequot, leaving her car at the shopping plaza until later. We cut through to Main Street and ride up Seaview to Hull. I don't see any cops along the way, and I suppose it's because they're all still occupied with Polky. At my place we get out of the pickup and she comes into my arms and I hold her. Then we go inside and sit at the kitchen table. I open a couple of beers and give her one.

"I hope Billy's okay," Niki says.

"I think he will be."

"It was *awful*, people shooting, cops chasing us."

"Yeah," I say. We fall silent then, and I listen to my mother's clock ticking on the wall behind me. Niki's frowning down at her hands.

"Do you still want to stay?" I say.

She looks up quick. Then she pushes back her chair.

We take turns in the bathroom, go into the big bedroom. We sit on the bed and Niki holds my hand again in both of hers. She looks down at our hands, waiting.

"I guess I need to tell you all about it," I say finally.

"Okay, Troy," she says.

We settle back on the pillows. Niki turns onto her side, puts her head on my chest. Her breath smells minty and clean, and I want to kiss her, but I start talking instead. My voice seems kind of rumbly. I run down the whole spring, how I got to where I am. I tell her about Polky trying to recruit me, and how I fended him off until I thought I had no other choice. Then how Polky changed his tune and said it would be one and done, we'd buy ourselves a year and go straight and see how it worked out. "And here's the thing," I say. "That can still happen. I know I said never again, but this is still the same deal. If I can find the basketball and get it to Polky, then I've got a chance. But we're in this together now." I shut up and wait, staring at the old tin ceiling in the faint light coming from the kitchen night light.

Niki takes her time. But finally she says, "I'm sorry, Troy."

I let my breath out. But I touch her cheek, so she won't take it the wrong way, because I really did mean what I said. "Okay," I say. "We'll just see what happens."

"I'll help all I can," she says.

"Okay." I hold her tight.

"But now I have to explain something," she says.

"No you don't. I understand."

"No." She puts her hand flat on my chest. "Listen, you remember when I was a kid, how I was. Well, after Stonie died I had no idea what to do. We'd made ourselves sort of alone, you know? And I didn't have anyone to talk to about it. But your mom went to the funeral and then came to see me afterwards. Did you know that?"

"No, she never told me that."

"She let me blubber all over her. She hugged me, Troy. It was like having a mother. After that's when I started coming over here again. I slept in your room upstairs sometimes. And one night when I was over here I decided to change. I wanted to be good enough to keep coming over. I wanted to pay her back. It was wicked hard, because I'd done whatever I wanted to for so long. I couldn't do it halfway, either, not with your mom caring about me." She squeezes me. "And I still have to be good enough for her."

"Okay," I say.

"I'm real sorry," she says.

"No, I get it."

We hold each other, and I think about her coming over here and my mother taking her in. It sounds like my mother. I get a little wet-eyed, thinking about her and Niki. I decide I'm glad we're going to do the right thing, no matter what happens, and I touch Niki so she knows everything's really okay, and she touches me back. We lie there holding each other and then it comes on me fast and I want her real bad, but I'm not brave enough to start anything and maybe she isn't, either. We just hold on and the wanting eases after a while and we're cozy together and we start to fade. I go in and out of it for some time and we don't move and then at some point we're asleep.

But we don't sleep all the way through the night. What we let settle away from us waits until we're asleep and rested and comes washing back stronger than ever. It wakes Niki first, and then I come to with her hand on me, and her lips on mine, and the kiss goes on until it's everything in the world. I'm still half asleep, but I realize she's gotten naked, and I wriggle out of my clothes and turn to feel her body against mine. She pushes me back, still kissing me, and then somehow she's all around me, perched above me, catching her breath, my palms smoothing up her sides, her hands gripping my wrists. And the two of us holding on until my mind scatters, and she shudders and we melt together, for who knows how long, and then we're ourselves again, breathing like we've been underwater. She floats off me onto her side and I look at her face and can't believe how sweet it is to be with her. We tell each other things, mostly about how dumb we were to let it take so long, and then we snuggle close and go back to sleep.

When we wake again its light outside and toasty in the bed and Niki is holding me and chuckling deep in her throat.

"What's so funny?" I say, my lips against her neck.

"I used to wish I was your sister," she says.

I feel her warmth under the covers and I wonder about it happening again. Niki's thinking along the same lines, I can tell. But we've slept too late, the light is too bright in the room, and before long it has dragged us back into the world with everyone else and the basketball out there somewhere in the canal.

Niki sighs and says, "We'd better get up, huh?"

"I suppose," I say.

We get out of bed and pull our clothes back on. We go into the kitchen and have coffee, holding hands, and then we put our cups in the sink and head outside. It's sunny, the creek sparkling, the big birds busy, the poor fish splashing. We walk down past the dock and the shags stir, watching us. We cross the field to the old mule path and walk slowly into the woods, her arm around my waist, mine around her shoulders, Niki careful in her work shoes. It's shady in the woods, cool and earthy-smelling. We follow the path to the old Hull graveyard, and stop there to look at the stones.

"All your folks," Niki says.

"Except two," I say.

"But they're really here," Niki says. "I can feel them."

"I hope they're not mad at me," I say.

"I think they're proud of you."

"I'll bet they're prouder of you."

Niki covers her mouth with her fingertips, shuts her eyes, leans against me. We wander around the old graveyard, looking at the tilting stones. We stand next to Sam the springer's small granite marker for a few minutes. Niki stands on her toes to kiss my cheek. Then we start off hiking up the canal. We cover the ground at a pretty good clip. I haven't walked up this far for a long while, and I expect it to be overgrown and tough going, but it isn't really all that bad. We hold back the briars for each other, and we walk together along the old path.

THIRTY-SEVEN

Okay, so I might as well end like I started: spring again, running my boat out of the bay toward Shag Island and Pequot Harbor, the first I've been back since I sold out.

Oh yeah, there was no fairy-tale ending.

I had to sell out.

There was really no way around it after we decided to do the right thing. But it wasn't as bad as it could have been. It turned out there was enough money to pay off my boat and buy a trailer and a couple of acres from Bobby Lawson. Part of the deal was Bobby coming to work as my sternman, and when the fishing picked up that fall I was able to keep him on. Now we're hoping things will stay in the right direction this year.

Don't get me wrong; I won't ever lose the ache from selling Hull Creek. But at least I ended up with a little salt water, and sometime in the future we'll have a decent home. It shouldn't take forever with both of us working. And it is nice to finish hauling and be almost home, Julie Marie was right about that. But of course it's Niki Harjula I'm going home to, which is why the new lettering on the boat:

Niki H

Owls Head, ME.

I'm alone on the boat, partly because Niki's working at the Rockland Credit Union today—all her little brochures back in place—and partly because I didn't know whether I wanted her along anyway. I kind of had to do this by myself.

I clear the ledge and look up at the little island where we used to have bonfires after big games, and then I look toward the landing. I can't say Pequot doesn't still grab at me. The park, the mountain, the boardwalk, the granite, the footbridge, the steeples. My old life.

The day I signed off on the deal was brutal.

We closed in Keith Zeiglaar's office, with our old school pictures still on the walls, with Trace White and Donald Hartley and various realtors and lawyers. Just thinking about Trace White's face and Hartley's phony sympathy is enough to piss me off at any given moment. But the price was quite a bit more than they had wanted to pay, thanks to one of Niki's swanky legal friends. She'd told me I could trust the guy, and she was right, he put it right to the little Pequot Savings and Loan gang: there was enough evidence of collusion that even if we couldn't win a court fight, we could do some real damage to their reputations. Especially with a former employee of the bank as a witness.

But no way in hell could I have done it except for Niki. I'd have gone down with the ship. I was able to agree to it because I realized I was trading my old life alone at Hull Creek for a new one with her somewhere else.

I clear the island and look at the old iron bridge. It's low tide and the water is rushing past the concrete brace in the middle of the creek. The creek looks the same from here. You can't see the new house, so you can't even tell that the old house is gone.

I putt in past Danny Brinker's marina—the little bastard—and pick my way through the sailboats to the landing. They're working on the schooner already: a college girl is high up on the mast, wearing a climbing rig like the phone company uses. Her knees are clamped onto the mast and she's brushing it with creosote. I feel a tug in my center and think that that's another thing that made things okay: having that back, having *that* with Niki.

I reverse engine and nose up to the float, where Freddie Linscott is scrubbing his launch down, pulling a big, dripping sponge out of a soapy bucket. Freddie saw me coming in, gave me the high sign, and then went back to work. Now he stops again as I jump to the float. He sits back on his haunches and says, "Hey there, Troy." I know he's thinking about me losing Hull Creek, but he doesn't say anything about it.

"How's it going, Freddie?"

"Finest kind," he says.

"Am I good here for an hour or so?"

"Be my guest."

I thank him, cross the walkway, and start up the gangway.

"Hey, you hear about Polky getting out?" Freddie calls.

"Oh, yeah." I stop and look back down at him.

"You seen him yet?"

"He came by," I say.

"So is he rehabilitated?"

I just laugh. Freddie waves and goes back to work. I continue up onto the boardwalk and down to Erky Jura's wharf. I follow the wharf to Seaview, passing the Ice Cream Shoppe and the little Mexican pizza joint and a couple of new businesses. Seagulls watch me from on all the roofs. I pass the realty office and look across at Cobb's, tempted to stop in for a beer. But maybe Polky will be there, and I don't feel like talking to him. Not that he holds anything against me. He even admitted he got us in over our heads, and he's grateful I charged down the hill and saved his skin. It was touch and go for a while, though. He spent time in intensive care at the Pen-Bay hospital because of the gunshot that took a piece of his liver. His ear has its V-notch, too, and goes with his claw pretty well.

Polky spent six months in jail after he got out of the hospital. They couldn't convict him of selling drugs, and they couldn't prove he was lying about a gun sale gone wrong (he'd brought his own pistol, but it had slipped too far under his seat and he couldn't reach it in time), but they threw everything they could at him: Possession of a loaded firearm in a vehicle, half an ounce of pot in his trunk, probation violation, too. They managed to tuck him away for a bit. They tried to get me to confess to being the guy who ran from the cruiser, but I held to my story and Niki backed me up—she said I'd done the right thing and that made fibbing okay—and they had no proof to the contrary. And my assault charges went away because there were witnesses who said I hadn't assaulted anyone. Taylor Miles was one of them. He surprised us by calling up and offering to help. He said he'd never liked what was going on. Taylor Miles was all right.

Polky got word to me from jail to stay clear, so it wasn't until he got out that we actually talked. He knew it was going to be bad news though, because he knew I'd lost the house. He came by on his Harley and looked at my trailer and made a face. I was sitting in an Adirondack in front of the door, reading one of the old man's books. He dismounted and said, "So tell me what happened." He had a prison haircut, he'd lost some weight, and his face was pale. He looked like a high school basketball player again.

We walked down to my little piece of water, and that's where I told him I'd let the stuff blow out the window while I was running away. He shook his head and looked out at Big Branch. I felt bad lying to him, but it wouldn't have served any useful purpose to tell him we found the basketball trapped under a blow-down hanging into the canal, brought the zip-locks back and burned them into a hard little lump in my woodstove.

Polky finally said, "At least they think the assholes took it." He explained that they'd thought from the police reports that the guys who shot him were in the vehicle that escaped.

Polky said that he guessed he'd just go back to fishing, if the catch stayed reasonable. But I have my doubts about that. For one thing, he owes his business associates. But also, before he left he was going on about *fucking swanks* and how it just wasn't fair that I had to move to *Owls Fucking Head* and live in a tin can when my family had built Hull Creek and lived there for *six fucking generations*.

"It sucks big-time, Troy-boy," Polky said, kicking at the gravel strip that passed for a beach at my new place.

"Yep," I said. What else could I say?

After a while we walked back to the trailer and he jumped on his bike and took off.

I stroll along Seaview Street and start up the slope with all the fancy houses. Just as I pass the yacht club, Eddy Cranberry comes shuffling out of the path from the green and into the street. He crosses and falls into step with me. I don't really mind, though. Being with Eddy is still sort of like being alone.

"Hey!" he says, and takes a slug of juice. He's not too ripe today. New overalls, I guess.

"Hey, Eddy," I say.

We climb on up the hill, my knees a little sore, and we turn onto Hull Street. Charlie Hamalainen's old yard is mowed and landscaped, and someone has cleared out the bushes that used to stand between his house and mine, so that there's just a long flat stretch, tilled, seeded, and covered with hay. There's a rectangular area staked off in that new part, and I figure that's for Donald Hartley's tennis court. There are young apple trees planted around, too, with beaver-guards and guy wires.

We walk down Hull, looking ahead at the new house. It's all gables and dormers, gray-shingled, with a widow's walk on top. Kind of a make-believe sea captain's house. The shingles flare out at the bottom into a skirt that goes all the way around.

We walk up the driveway and see that they're still finishing some of the details: lanterns on the driveway, wrought-iron benches, a big deck on the same side where mine used to be. It's Saturday, and nobody's working, but from what I understand it'll be ready to go by the time summer is in full swing.

The willow is still there, and all the tall ashes and the birches. It squeezes my heart hard to look at them, and I close my eyes for a moment. Eddy stops beside me, and I hear the juice gurgle. I open my eyes and we walk on down the driveway—tall hedges, smooth black tar—and past the willow. We pass the big birch, the little bog opposite the wide part of the creek. They haven't done any work along here: it looks the same as ever. Even the old dock is still standing.

Eddy and I walk out onto the dock. There are dozens of shags in the creek, and seagulls hanging around whimpering and bleating, and there are alewives splashing circles in the water. Across, the phlox is bright along the bank and there are white blossoms on the apple trees and scattered on the ground.

The shags keep an eye on us, and when we sit down on the dock, they start milling around, craning their necks. When I suddenly raise my arms—and when Eddy throws his up, too—they burst into motion, scrambling into a long take-off run, smacking the water with their feet, beating their wings, filling the whole of Hull Creek with the sound of their applause. They fly off along the surface: ten, then twenty, then a hundred or more. I stand up on the dock, and Eddy stands up beside me. I raise my hands above my head, and Eddy shoves his into the air, too.

"Thank you!" I say in my best Elvis voice.

"Hey!" Eddy says.

"Thank you very much!" I shout.

The applause dies out and we watch the straining shags and the swirling, crabby seagulls, and then Eddy points across the creek at a fish hawk, holding his wings wide as he settles on a tiny bobbing perch on a tall ash. He's something, with his hooked beak, his white vest and brown jacket. He's pretty goddamn *stunning*, to use Polky's word. He steps around until he finds the right spot, and then he settles. Pretty soon he stops swaying.